THE PAGANINI CURSE

The Paganini Curse

GISELLE M. STANCIC

iUniverse, Inc.
Bloomington

The Paganini Curse

iUniverse books may be ordered through booksellers or by contacting:

iUniverse
1663 Liberty Drive
Bloomington, IN 47403
www.iuniverse.com
1-800-Authors (1-800-288-4677)

ISBN: 978-1-4759-6159-1 (sc)
ISBN: 978-1-4759-6161-4 (hc)
ISBN: 978-1-4759-6160-7 (e)

Library of Congress Control Number: 2012921232

Printed in the United States of America

iUniverse rev. date: 1/9/2013

For M, N,
and
little m

Chapter 1

AURORA LEWIS HUGGED HER black violin case closer to her body, waiting on the corner of Fifty-Seventh Street and Seventh Avenue for a break in the chaos of honking motor cars. Every week the noise and confusion got worse, with more of those smoking four-wheel contraptions crowding out the few horse-drawn carts left in New York City—automobiles driven by fools with no sense about going too fast or staying on the right side of the road.

Father said they were working on a signaling tower for the intersection, but Mother wasn't about to believe that some newfangled device was going to bring order to the bedlam. To her the street noise was just another reason to move from Grandmother's lovely flat in the Osborne Building to the edge of nowhere on the Upper West Side, into one of those fancy apartment suites in the Dakota.

The Dakota was simply *the* place to live in 1911, Mother was quick to remind them. But fifteen-year-old Aurora wasn't expecting to share an elevator with the Rockefellers anytime soon, not on Father's accountant salary. Besides, as far as she was concerned, this was the center of the universe. Just a five-minute walk to Carnegie Hall, and her Saturday morning music lessons with Professor Schmieder.

Brrr. She stomped her feet to keep warm. January's bitter temperatures cut through her wool coat and red leather gloves. Not to mention that in her rush out the door she'd forgotten her hat. Her wavy auburn hair would be a tangled mess, and she could hear Mother now, scolding her about catching her death of cold in this weather.

But she wasn't about to get sick, not before the most important week of her life. Maud Powell was finally here.

The newspapers called her the "First Lady of the American Violin." To Aurora, Maud Powell was the perfect combination of talent and beauty, with her upswept dark brown hair, flowing evening gown, and virtuoso violin technique. Ever since Father had brought home one of Miss Powell's records to play on their Victrola, it had been Aurora's dream to see her idol in person.

She and Grandmother had tickets to hear Miss Powell play with the New York Philharmonic tomorrow afternoon. But more important, Aurora was going to be in Miss Powell's master class next Saturday in Carnegie Hall, where she would play a solo for the famous violinist in front of the other students and an audience.

She'd just found out before the holidays that she had been chosen for the class, and this morning would be her first chance to share the news with Professor Schmieder. With all her practicing, and playing her teacher's arrangement for solo violin of the Paganini "Romanze," she was certain she would make an unforgettable impression on Miss Powell.

The sound of crunching metal brought the traffic to a sudden halt. In a blur, one of those crazy bicycle messengers sped past her down the avenue. He must have startled an unsuspecting driver, causing him to swerve into the path of another automobile. But only bent fenders and bruised egos seemed to be the casualties, given how quickly both men jumped out of their cars and started throwing punches. As for the pedaling menace, he just kept on going, not even noticing the ruckus caused in his wake.

Aurora used the temporary lull to cross the street, trying not to listen to the salty language that would have had her mother washing her ears out with soap. Gripping her violin case in one hand and lifting up her long green skirt with the other, she stepped around the sink holes and horse piles dotting the rutted avenue, careful not to scuff her polished black leather boots. She was nearly across when a revving engine backfired behind her. Aurora leapt to the curb and let out a few salty words of her own. What would Mother think now?

Safe on the other side of the street, she found herself elbow-to-elbow with people streaming out of Carnegie Hall. Since it was too early for a concert, she figured Mr. Carnegie must be holding one of his peace conferences again.

Father thought Andrew Carnegie was a crackpot for promoting something called a "League of Nations" to solve the world's problems. Aurora didn't know much about politics—that was men's business, after all. But Mr. Carnegie couldn't be completely off-key. Just look at the beautiful music hall that carried his name.

The elegant building rose above New York's grimy streets, its classic brick and brownstone exterior graced with tall, arched windows. When Mr. Carnegie built the hall back in 1891, the critics said he would never get an audience all the way uptown for a concert. Twenty years later, the city had grown up around the place.

Aurora worked her way through the crowd to the building's entrance and then into the lobby to the elevator going up to the Carnegie Towers. The Towers gave musicians and artists inexpensive studio space to rent, and all the inspiration they needed from the performances going on next door in the concert hall. Sometimes when Maestro Mahler demanded an extra Saturday rehearsal for the Philharmonic, Aurora could even hear the music coming in through the heater vents in Professor Schmieder's studio.

"Fourth floor, please," she said to the elevator attendant, a stooped little man obviously undersized for his wrinkled brown uniform.

"Yes, miss," he said, his eyes never looking up from the floor.

She clung to the railing as the narrow box shimmied its way upward, whining even more than usual as if the cables were going to break. When they finally arrived on the fourth floor, Aurora exited in a hurry. Now if she could just get past the drama school without being noticed.

Most lesson days she enjoyed the good-hearted bantering with the young men from the Academy of Dramatic Arts, on break from their play rehearsal or acting class. Especially cute little Eddie Robinson, with his bushy hair and tough-guy attitude. She liked him ever so much better than Bill Powell, who was all slicked back and smirking, forever bragging about how he was going to be in the moving pictures like the ones they were showing down on Forty-Second Street. As if being in those short ditties was ever going to be more important than acting on the stage.

Then there was the third member of their troupe, Theo Eckstein. Tall, gangly, with a pale complexion and rimless oval glasses, he always wore a sensible gray sweater and dark blue trousers to complete his studious, almost invisible look.

But today she didn't have time to chat with the boys. She wanted to get to her lesson early to tell Professor Schmieder the good news about the master class with Miss Powell.

She'd almost made it past the academy when a long wolf whistle stopped her in her tracks.

"Hey there, beautiful. Not even a 'hello' for us?"

Aurora spun around and took a few steps toward the young man leaning out from the school's doorway.

"Shh, Eddie." She drew her finger to her lips. "You know Professor Schmieder doesn't like it when you boys make too much noise out here."

Seeing that she was still wearing her gloves, she slipped them off and tucked them into her coat pocket.

Eddie turned his head away. "Hey, Bill, Aurora's here. But she doesn't want to associate with us unsophisticates no more."

When Bill joined Eddie, Aurora couldn't help giggling. They must have been rehearsing an Arabian melodrama. Eddie was dressed as if he'd just stepped off a pirate boat, with bright purple pantaloons and a jeweled scabbard slung over his shoulder. A scraggly mustache and black eye patch finished off his buccaneer costume. Bill wore a long white robe and a turban perched lopsided on his head.

A few seconds later, Theo appeared behind them. As usual, he was hanging back a step, still in his no-nonsense street clothes. While the other boys talked about Theo becoming a great director someday, Aurora could hardly believe such a shy fellow would be able to command the attention of a group of rowdy actors.

"Aurora, you're hurting our feelings." Eddie reached for her violin case, his hand covering hers. "Here, let me hold your fiddle for you. We wait all week for the chance to see you."

"That's right, Aurora," said Bill, taking hold of her other hand. "Forget about that old grouch and spend the day with us. We think you're the prettiest girl in Manhattan."

"Come now." She blushed. "There are plenty of pretty girls right here at the academy."

"Not like you," said Eddie, looking at her admiringly.

"Not like you," Theo repeated softly, surprising them all by joining in the conversation.

"Well, well. I think our Theo is smitten," said Bill. "And why shouldn't he be, with your lovely green eyes and all that gorgeous Titian hair? Aurora could be the fair maiden in your first moving picture, couldn't she, Theo? And I'll be the hero who rescues her from the snake pits of the Yucatan."

Aurora ignored Bill's puffery to check Professor Schmieder's studio door at the end of the corridor. Odd, it was still closed. Usually he would have it open for her a few minutes before the start of her lesson.

"Don't worry," said Eddie. "Your teacher's probably still busy with the student that went in earlier this morning."

"Yes, she was a fine-looking lady," said Bill, smiling at the memory of her.

What? Professor Schmieder had a student come in before her? He always said his best teaching was done first thing in the morning, and he saved his Saturdays especially for her. Now another girl—no, a fine-looking lady—had moved into her spot on the professor's schedule?

She pulled away from the boys. "You're going to get me in trouble. I'll talk with you later."

"Play nice for the teacher," Eddie called after her.

As Aurora drew nearer to Professor Schmieder's studio, she realized the door wasn't completely closed after all. She pressed her ear to the wooden panel, expecting to hear his new protégé rattling off the cadenza from the Mendelssohn concerto or some other virtuoso solo. But the studio was quiet.

Maybe Professor Schmieder was telling his new favorite student about how she would be the first woman concertmaster in the New York Philharmonic. Wait a minute; that was Aurora's destiny. She leaned into the door accidentally, or maybe not so accidentally, and opened it a little wider.

She hesitated, expecting to hear the professor's low voice on the other side. But there was still no sound.

As nonchalantly as she could, Aurora announced her arrival by knocking on the door.

"Professor Schmieder, it's me, Aurora. I just wanted to let you know I'm here."

No response.

Now that was strange. Even if she irritated the professor, which she did on occasion with her excessive chattering, as he called it, he still wouldn't give her the silent treatment.

She knocked louder, calling out his name again. Finally, unable to contain her curiosity, Aurora stuck her head around the door to take a quick peek.

The professor's studio was furnished more like a Victorian sitting parlor than a place for music lessons. A high-backed, floral-print sofa and matching chair were set in the middle of the room, although Aurora couldn't remember ever sitting on the stiff cushions. The deep-red wallpaper was flocked in velvet and ornately framed paintings of the professor's homeland in Bavaria decorated the room.

With no sight or sound of her teacher, Aurora let herself in. On the far side of the studio stood Professor Schmieder's grand piano, which he sometimes played to accompany her during her lesson. And his most treasured possession, his Gagliano violin, was safe in its black case, lying on the piano bench.

The professor's handwritten manuscript of the Paganini "Romanze" was set out on the carved wooden music stand if they needed to review the markings. Everything looked normal, except …

A cold blast of wind slapped her cheek. The window behind the piano, which was usually covered by heavy curtains, stood wide open with the drapes pulled back. Frigid air filled the room with every gust from the outside.

What was the professor thinking? In the two years she had been studying with him, he'd always kept his studio warm. Almost stiflingly so, to ease the discomfort of his rheumatism. Aurora set her violin case down by the door and hurried over to shut the window. Moving around the piano, she noticed dark red spots on the lower end of the keyboard. She couldn't believe Professor Schmieder would allow anyone to soil the polished ivory keys.

Reaching to close the window, she could hear loud voices coming from the alleyway below. Probably those boys who dug through the garbage bins looking for something to sell or, God forbid, something to eat. Aurora leaned out the window to see what was going on.

The street kids were down there all right, but they weren't going through the trash. The boys were huddled together, nudging at something with their boots. Then one of the hooligans started pointing at the Towers building.

"There she is," he shouted. "She's up there."

The rest of the boys turned to take a look.

Aurora did as well, but all she saw were closed windows on her right and an empty fire escape off to her left.

"The girl with the red hair." The boy gestured excitedly. "In the window."

Aurora stared down at her coat collar, covered in jumbled curls. She didn't like being called a redhead, but she knew he was talking about her.

"She's the one that done it. She done pushed him."

What was he talking about? Pushed who?

"Come on, fellas. Let's catch her before she gets away."

The gang quickly disbanded and started running down the alley. After they left, Aurora could see what they had been poking at on the ground. In horror, she recognized Professor Schmieder's shock of white hair and the red-and-green plaid scarf he wore when he was ailing in the cold weather. But what turned her stomach was the peculiar way his legs twisted away from his body, as if he was a rag doll and someone had pulled on him from opposite directions.

Aurora grabbed the window sill to steady herself, but her grip slipped on the wet, sticky surface. Turning her hand over, she stared at the blood smeared across her palm. Instinctively she started wiping her hand on her coat. But the more feverishly she tried to rub out the stain, the deeper it soaked into her skin.

Aurora didn't remember screaming, or brushing her bloody fingers across her forehead. Or hitting the dissonant chord on the piano as she sank to the floor. She didn't remember anything except the color of red.

And thinking, *How will I ever explain this to Mother?*

Chapter 2

AURORA'S EYES FLUTTERED OPEN, trying to focus on the strange faces hovering above her. A swarthy pirate with a long mustache and black eye patch stood next to a sultan of Sudan struggling to keep his turban from sliding off his head. Had she woken up on some faraway island never to see Mother and Father again?

Or maybe a witch had cast her into a deep sleep. Aurora closed her eyes to reverse the spell. Then she started hearing voices around her, but they weren't speaking in some strange, foreign language. They were talking in plain English, with a familiar from New York accent.

"She's fainted again," said one of them.

"Maybe she's dead," said another.

Someone grabbed her hand and started feeling around under the cuff of her coat sleeve. Now that was too much. She wouldn't have anyone touching her without her permission.

"Stop that!" Aurora's eyes opened wide as she sat up straight, stunning the room into silence.

She could see that she was in Professor Schmieder's studio, seated on the fine sofa that he never used. Of course, she was here for her violin lesson. But why were all these other people around, and where was her teacher? She searched the faces of the sheik and the buccaneer. Standing behind them was a group of ragtag boys with dirty cheeks and tattered collars. Blankly she turned from one to the next until her gaze finally rested on someone she recognized. Theo Eckstein, the boy from the drama school. Their eyes locked and she mouthed the words, "What's going on?"

Theo stepped forward, brushing the onlookers aside so he could sit down next to her.

"Do you feel all right?" he asked.

Aurora nodded.

"You gave us quite a fright there," said Theo.

The pirate stepped in to take a closer look.

"Darn right you did," he said.

Aurora started to laugh. The Jolly Roger look-alike was Eddie Robinson wearing a silly costume. And the Arab prince next to him was his classmate, Bill Powell.

She laughed even harder.

"Aurora." Theo shyly took her hand. "You've had a shock. These boys say they saw you with the professor."

"That's right, she done him in." A scrawny young fellow stepped forward. She knew it wasn't polite to notice, but he had the biggest ears she'd ever seen, sticking out from underneath his red wool cap.

"She gave the old man a push." The kid demonstrated to the delight of his buddies. "Right out the window."

The street urchins doubled over in amusement.

"Splat on the ground."

Aurora stiffened, now remembering the open window and Professor Schmieder's mangled body sprawled in the alley.

She buried her head in Theo's shoulder. His soft wool sweater swallowed her tears, and she felt his arm carefully wrap around her.

"You fellows, all of you, get out of here."

She had never heard Theo raise his voice before.

"Eddie, get them into the hallway."

His command emptied the studio.

"It's better now," Theo whispered. "They've gone away."

Aurora tentatively looked around. The only other person left was Bill, obviously miffed that Theo had grabbed the prime spot next to the girl.

"Wait a minute," said Bill, pulling off his unruly headpiece and running out of the room.

Theo helped Aurora sit back against the cushions. "The police will be here any minute and they'll want to talk to you."

"But why me?" she asked.

"Just a few questions, I'm sure. You see, those boys seem to think you had something to do with the professor's fall."

Bill was back, the end of his unwound turban now soaked with water.

"We need to clean you up before the cops get here." He knelt in front of her and wiped her forehead and then showed her the red stain on the material.

"My goodness," said Aurora. "I must look a fright."

"You're as beautiful as always," said Bill, gently cleaning her hands while Theo looked on. Aurora knew he wouldn't try to compete with Bill's suave manner.

"What else?" Bill looked around, now taking charge of the situation. "We found you over there with your violin, by the piano."

Aurora turned to look at the bloodied keys.

"Don't worry," said Bill. "I'll take care of it."

"No, you won't." A burly uniformed policeman stood in the doorway. "Not if you know what's good for you." His warning, wrapped in a thick Irish brogue, left no room for misunderstanding.

Bill's swagger collapsed as he sought out a dark corner of the studio. At the same time, Theo's arm noticeably dropped from around Aurora's shoulder. So much for her brave defenders.

"Now, young lady." The officer hovered over her, blocking her view of anything else in the room except for the shiny belt buckle clasped over his big stomach. "I'm Detective O'Shea. Why don't you tell me what went on here this morning? We understand that you were with the professor." The policeman cleared his throat. "Before he tumbled out the window."

"But I just got here," said Aurora. "I didn't even see Professor Schmieder until I looked down into the alley."

The detective shook his head.

"Miss, those boys say they saw you and the professor in the window together," he said. "So why don't you tell me what really happened?"

He can't be serious, thought Aurora. *How could he believe a story from a bunch of hoodlums over what she was telling him?*

"Miss." The policeman leaned forward to look her in the eye, his foul breath wafting over her. Up close, she could see the hairs inside his bulbous red nose, and the waggling folds of his double chin as he talked.

"I'm not going to wait forever," he said. "Tell me the truth."

The detective was frightening her. Aurora swallowed hard, blinking to keep back the tears starting to well in her eyes.

Then all at once, Theo's arm was around her again.

"Detective," he said, his voice two octaves too high.

"Detective O'Shea," he said again, back to his normal tone. "Miss Lewis is quite upset over what happened. Might I suggest that I make sure she gets home safely and you can talk with her there? After she's had a chance to recover from the shock."

The policeman took a step back, eying Theo suspiciously.

"What's your name?" he asked gruffly.

Aurora felt Theo's body tense up.

"Theo Eckstein."

"What's your association with this young lady?" O'Shea asked. "Miss Lewis, is it?"

Theo spoke haltingly. "She's my—what I mean is ..."

Oh no, thought Aurora. *He'd been doing so well up to now.*

"She's my fiancée," he blurted.

From the corner of the room, Bill gasped.

Aurora dared not take a peek at Theo. How did he ever come up with such a story?

"Is that so, miss?" the detective asked. "I don't see a ring on your finger."

Aurora felt Theo's chest expand into his gray sweater.

"We're keeping the engagement quiet, sir." He assumed the assured voice she had heard earlier. "Until I can have a talk with her father and get his approval. She's still very young."

Theo's confidence was building.

"I'm responsible for Miss Lewis's well-being, and I need to get her home to her parents' care. She lives just down the block, in the Osborne Building."

Wait a minute, thought Aurora, still keeping a straight face. *How does he know where I live?*

"She'll be able to answer your questions there, in the presence of her mother and father," Theo went on. "That might look better in your report."

The detective started to object but decided against it. The New York police were known for their bullying tactics. Perhaps this large-sized cop knew better than to blunder into another situation for the scandal sheets.

"All right," said O'Shea. "I'll go down and take a look at the body in the alley. I'll send Sergeant Daley up here to get all your names and addresses." He turned to Bill. "You too, Sinbad."

"Yes, sir," said Bill, although Aurora could barely hear him.

"Miss Lewis, I'll be coming by your family's apartment later this afternoon. I have to finish here then go over to Sixth Avenue to take care of a woman they found drowned in her bathtub." He chuckled. "Only there wasn't any water in it."

Aurora grimaced. What an awful man, doing an awful job.

"Tell your parents I'll be there after four o'clock." Detective O'Shea's puffy face was right next to hers. "And I don't want any funny business, like you not being at home when I come around."

"Miss Lewis will cooperate fully, sir," said Theo. "Once I see she's back to being herself," he added, hugging her closer for good measure.

Aurora fought the urge to wriggle away from him. Maybe Theo was starting to enjoy his role as her protector a bit too much.

Chapter 3

IF THE DOORMAN AT the Osborne had any questions about the serious-looking young man accompanying Aurora home later than usual from her violin lesson, he was discreet enough to hide his interest.

"Hello, Miss Lewis," he said, holding open the front door for them.

"Hello, Charles." Aurora quickly stepped inside, not offering to introduce Theo or explain why he was carrying her violin case.

She'd nearly made it through the lobby before noticing Theo was no longer behind her. He was standing just inside the door, staring up at the vaulted ceiling covered with shimmering mosaics. After years of going in and out of the building, she'd forgotten how impressive the Osborne could be to a visitor. Still, she couldn't dawdle on a day like today.

"Come on, Theo," she called out.

Charles, ever the gentleman, turned the other way. But not before a faint smile crossed his lips.

"Wait a minute." Theo pointed to the blue-and-white tiled walls. "Look at all the detail in these patterns." Then he tapped his foot on the floor. "And this is imported Italian red marble. It's like you're living in a palace."

"Theo," said Aurora.

"You know," he said, walking slowly toward her, taking it all in. "I'm something of a student of New York architecture. From the street, the Osborne is one the best examples of Renaissance revival in the city. But I've never been inside before."

Is that why he had insisted on walking in with her, instead of parting ways out on the curb? And she'd thought it was because he was concerned about her getting home safely.

"I read that Thomas Osborne was a stone contractor," said Theo. "He wanted to give the residents of his building the feeling they were living in a place as impressive as any millionaire's."

He stopped in front of one of the lobby's grand fireplaces and pointed to an alabaster cameo above the mantel. "Just look at this lady with the lyre. She could belong in a mansion on Riverside Drive."

Another time Aurora would have probably enjoyed the art lesson. In turn, she could have shown Theo the building's hidden staircases and private window wells, where she sometimes stole away when her parents' "discussions" got too loud in the apartment. But she didn't have time to meander. She still couldn't believe Professor Schmieder was dead, and now she had to figure out a way to tell her parents.

"Your flat must be lovely." Theo was rambling on. "I've heard the rooms have fifteen-foot ceilings."

"The apartment belongs to my grandmother," she said. "She lets us live with her, since Father is her only child and she likes having us around for the company."

"Does her place have the hand-carved woodwork from South America?"

"Theo, my violin, please." Aurora stopped at the foot of the dark oak staircase leading to the higher floors. She could manage the rest of the way by herself. Explaining why a strange boy had walked her home would be too much for her parents to handle.

"Are you sure you don't want me to go up with you?" he asked. "Your fainting spell gave us all a scare, and I did say I would be responsible for you."

"Thank you, Theo. But I'm not a child," she said, raising her voice louder than she intended. Charles the doorman turned his head slightly in their direction but remained silent.

Her voice dropped to a whisper. "How did you come up with that story about us being engaged, anyway? I've never heard of anything so preposterous."

"I wanted to give you some time to collect your thoughts, and it was the best I could do on the spot," said Theo. "You could be in real trouble, Aurora. You're going need to some help."

She looked into his eyes. There wasn't a hint of trying to boss her around, only a quiet determination to make his point clear. But she wasn't about to tell him that she was just as worried about everything that had gone on today.

"I can take care of myself," she said curtly.

"All right, I get the hint," said Theo. "But promise me you're going to talk to your parents, first thing."

Aurora nodded. She wasn't looking forward to that conversation.

"Then on your own, spend some time thinking about Professor Schmieder," he said. "Do you know anyone who might have been angry with him, or who he didn't get along with?"

"I hardly knew the professor," she said. "I mean, except for my lesson once a week."

"That could be all you need. Maybe he said something unusual, or you saw something out of place in his studio. Don't try to decide if it's important or not. In the meantime, I'll see what the fellas and I can come up with."

"Bill and Eddie … and you would do that for me?"

"Absolutely." He smiled. "It's not every day we get to rescue a real damsel in distress."

It turned out Theo was a good-looking young man when he wasn't being so serious.

"But how? I mean, when will I see you again?" She was embarrassed to ask such a forward question, but Theo didn't seem to mind.

"The guys and I will be at the Oak Room in the Plaza Hotel this afternoon," he said. "Try to meet us there by half past two. Then you'll still be able to get back home in time before Detective O'Shea comes around."

Aurora cringed. A policeman showing up at their front door. Mother will need her smelling salts.

"But once I tell my parents, they'll be watching me like hawks," she said. "I'll never get out of the apartment."

"Do your best." Theo handed over the violin case. "We'll be waiting for you." He paused. "I'll be waiting for you."

Without another word, he turned and headed back through the lobby. After thanking Charles for opening the door for him, Theo was out into the city.

To her surprise, Aurora wished she was going with him.

Chapter 4

AURORA TIPTOED INTO THE apartment. She tucked her violin case behind the coat stand near the front door and hung up her jacket, taking care to fold it to hide the red stain.

Her parents and grandmother must still be in the kitchen after their Saturday lunch. Father was probably poring over the business section of the newspaper, and sneaking a look at the racing sheets, while Mother was absorbed in her latest home-decorating catalog from Macy's. Grandmother would be nodding off in the corner with her knitting, not having made much progress on the wool scarf she had been working on for Aurora since last summer.

Leaning against the wall to unlace her boots, she thought about how she could tell her parents what happened this morning. There was always the direct approach.

"Mother, Father. Professor Schmieder fell from his studio window before my lesson today. And these silly boys told the police I had something to do with it."

That would send Mother into a tizzy.

"A detective will be coming by later this afternoon to ask me a few questions."

That would send Father into a tirade about the police having nothing better to do than harass law-abiding citizens in their own homes.

On second thought, maybe she should just avoid the situation altogether. She could take her violin and disappear out the front door, never to be seen or heard from again. After all, she still had her Christmas money. With that she could buy a train ticket, although she wasn't sure how far three dollars would take her. Along the way she could play her violin and collect coins in her case, like the musicians in Central Park when the weather was good. Maybe she could make enough in tips to get all the way to California. In one of her school books, she'd read it was sunny out there all year long.

Naturally she would miss Mother and Father and especially dear Grandmother. But sometimes sacrifices had to be made.

There was Theo, too, and of course, Bill and Eddie. She would stop by the Plaza Hotel just to let them know she was leaving. She wondered how Theo would take the news. Then she wondered why Theo's reaction now seemed important to her.

Aurora was so deep in thought she didn't hear the footsteps coming toward her until her mother's voice was nearly in her ear.

"Aurora, what are you doing out here with one boot off and one boot on?" Mother shook her head in disapproval. "Daughter's been daydreaming again, Winston."

Aurora's father, barely visible behind his ample wife in their narrow entry hall, let out a familiar sigh.

"Why are you so late coming home from your lesson?" asked Mother. "We were starting to think you had taken the long way again."

Aurora opened her mouth to speak, but as usual, her mother didn't give her a chance.

"Never mind, at least you're here," she said. "You know we don't like to leave your grandmother by herself."

Aurora now noticed that instead of her Saturday day dress, Mother was wearing a stylish red jacket over a navy pleated skirt, and her black hair was pinned back with the jeweled comb Father had given her for Christmas.

"Did you forget?" asked Mother. "We're going over to the soirée at the Wentworths' and look at the new painting they just bought from the Stieglitz Gallery."

What a stroke of luck. Mother had been talking about the Wentworths' party all week long.

"It's one of those modern pieces by a painter named Arthur Dove," said Mother. "I heard they paid a fortune for it."

Estelle Wentworth was an acquaintance of Mother's from the Metropolitan Museum Ladies' Club. Why her mother had been invited to join was a mystery, given that she had little appreciation for the arts and their social status was decidedly middle class. Aurora guessed that a large donation from Grandmother likely had something to do with Mother's new circle of friends.

"But most of all, I'm dying to see their apartment." Mother was droning on. "Estelle was telling me that she has one room all done in Chinese silk tapestries and porcelain vases. Her husband even brought back a rosewood chaise from his last trip to the Orient, like they used to carry the emperor in."

She gave her husband a long look.

"Not that we would ever have anything so exotic around here."

Poor Father just responded by rolling his eyes behind his glasses. Dressed in his dark blue suit and bow tie, he took his trusty gray overcoat from the rack and wrapped a gray scarf around his neck.

"Winston, my fur, please," said Mother.

She stepped back so he could drape a silver fox stole over her shoulders.

"Take care of your grandmother, Aurora," said Father.

"Yes," said Mother. "She's dottier than usual today."

Father chose to ignore the remark.

"We'll be back by four," he said, "if we can't get out of there any earlier."

"Winston," said Mother. "Don't you remember we talked about making a good impression?"

"All right, Marguerite," he said. "I'll try to be polite."

For once, Aurora was glad Mother had gotten her way. That would give her enough time to get to the Plaza and back, and for her parents to be home for Detective O'Shea's visit.

Oh no, the detective. She should say something.

"Mother, Father," she started.

"Winston, my hat!" Mother touched her bare head in a panic.

"It's right here." Father handed her a purple velvet bonnet trimmed with ostrich feathers.

"I don't know," she said, checking in the mirror. "Maybe I should wear the one with the satin bow. It goes better with my hair."

Aurora tried again. "Mother, I need to talk to you."

"For heaven's sake, Marguerite." Father put his foot down. "That bird's nest you've got on looks fine. Let's leave before I change my mind, and we don't go at all."

With that, they were out the door. Aurora never had a chance to tell them about Professor Schmieder or the police. Goodness, she was going to have even more explaining to do when they got home.

Never mind, Aurora told herself. At least she would have some time to think about the professor before meeting the boys. She'd do that after she made Grandmother a nice cup of tea, to lull her into her midday nap.

Aurora gently placed the needle down on the record spinning on the Victrola player. She'd been listening to Miss Powell's recordings, hoping the music would settle her mind enough so that she could come up with some information about the professor. In her family's cozy sitting room, comforted with a hot chocolate and the warmth from the fireplace, Aurora didn't have any excuses for distractions. Even Grandmother, happily snoozing in her rocking chair, wasn't cause for concern, despite Mother's warning.

But while she was listening to Miss Powell's enchanting rendition of Grieg's "To Spring," and her charming arrangement of Mozart's "Minuet in D," all Aurora could think of was the professor's body being poked at by those thugs in the alley.

Then she made the mistake of playing Miss Powell's haunting recording of the Schumann "Reverie." The shock of Professor Schmieder's death must have finally hit her, and Aurora couldn't hold back the tears. They were mostly for her teacher, but there were also a few for herself. Her life had been so simple until this morning. Practicing her violin, going to her lessons, playing in the master class. Now everything was topsy-turvy.

Even changing the record to a harmless Chopin waltz was cause for a few sniffles. Professor Schmieder sometimes used to play a quick ditty on the piano to liven up her lesson. Something light and pleasant like a waltz or a jig, or even a few bars from a popular song like "Alexander's Ragtime Band." That always surprised her, given the professor's condescending attitude toward anything so obviously working class.

If she could sum up Professor Schmieder, it was as if in his own mind he was still living in his beloved Heidelberg while being safely cocooned in his teaching studio above the crass New York City streets. But that's where he ended up, surrounded by the strangers he loathed.

The Empire grandfather clock in the dining room chimed twice. It was already two o'clock. Aurora lifted the needle from the record. She had to leave now or she'd be late for the Plaza.

She dropped a silent kiss on top of her grandmother's head and thought she saw the elderly lady's eyes quiver. But she didn't stir.

"I'll be back soon," Aurora whispered. "Don't worry."

Chapter 5

As Aurora turned the corner from Fifty-Eighth Street onto Fifth Avenue, the grand dame of New York's social scene appeared before her. Simply known as "The Plaza," the hotel was the most famous place in the city to see and be seen.

Towering nineteen stories above Grand Army Plaza at the southeast edge of Central Park, the Plaza Hotel exuded the elegance of upper-class New York. Built in the style of a medieval French chateau, the hotel boasted a row of colorful flags that waved in the brisk wind above the stained glass entrance. Doormen dressed in dark green overcoats with polished silver buttons greeted the high-society matrons arriving in their private motor coaches. Men in top hats emerged from the hotel smoking fine cigars and boasting of their latest triumphs in the stock market, while impatient visitors from faraway places instructed the bell captains on how to handle their mounds of luggage.

Aurora had heard stories about the hotel's gold-plated fixtures and rare antique furnishings, a true "heaven on earth." She would have a chance to see for herself if the indoor paradise was real.

Slipping through the gilded front doors on the coattails of a bellhop barely able to hang on to the leash of a rambunctious Great Dane, Aurora found herself transported into the world of nobility, American style. Every square inch of the lobby reflected the rewards of wealth. From the elaborate crystal chandeliers to the floor-to-ceiling mirrors, Aurora's eyes couldn't take in all the glitter and glamour. Swept along with the bustling flow of hotel guests, her boots sank into the thick Persian carpets woven in geometric designs.

But all that didn't hold a candle to what captured Aurora's attention on the other side of the lobby. A palm grove was growing in the middle of the New York winter. The sight of the tall, slender green fronds reaching up to the atrium's glass ceiling delighted her cold-weather sensibilities, while the heavy fragrance of potted hibiscus intoxicated her senses. Small tables were interleaved among the tropical foliage, each with seating for two or three ladies in wide-brimmed hats having their afternoon tea. Waiters in starched, white linen jackets dodged around them, carrying platters of delicate finger sandwiches and steaming pots of England's finest.

Drawn toward the oasis, Aurora's gaze fell upon a small party near the front of the dining area. A mother, smartly dressed in a pale-pink winter suit with a wide fur-trimmed collar and matching cuffs, was scolding her young son as she pointed to an assortment of French pastries set out before them. Standing near the table was a girl about Aurora's age, with a dour look on her face as she tried to ignore the fuss between her mother and little brother. To Aurora's amazement, the girl wasn't dressed in the usual corseted suit and heavy boots. Instead she wore a loose-fitting tunic made of blue plaid fabric that, heaven forbid, revealed her legs just above her ankles. What was the world coming to, when someone could go out in a dress that looked like a nightgown?

The girl, noticing she was being stared at, looked straight back at Aurora and stuck out her tongue. Well! Dressed like a bohemian and acting like one, too.

Then from behind one of the palm trees, Aurora heard the sound of a violinist tuning his instrument. What, they had live music here, too? A few seconds later, a man in a dark suit stepped into view, playing a jaunty tune she recognized from the operetta, *The Pirates of Penzance*. The society ladies kept right on with their talking as the violinist wandered among the tables, taking care to avoid the scurrying waiters while never losing a beat or landing on a misplaced note. Aurora wondered how a musician's talent could be squandered on such an unappreciative audience. Didn't they realize how much practice it took to play so well?

"Miss." A man's voice interrupted her ruminations. "Seating for one?"

Aurora looked to her left, into the frowning face of the Palm Court's host, who was holding out a menu and expecting an answer.

"Miss, are you here for tea?"

"I was just listening to the music," said Aurora. "He's very good."

"If you're dining with us this afternoon, you can listen all you want. Otherwise, you'll have to move along."

Since when was music being played in public only for the wealthy to enjoy? And they weren't even listening. Aurora was about to speak her mind when she felt a hand on her shoulder and heard a familiar voice.

"Miss Lewis, your table is ready for you in the Oak Room," said Theo. "We don't want to keep the others waiting."

"But I was just about to tell this man—"

"Excuse us, sir." Theo started to steer Aurora away from the manager, who watched them with a moment's curiosity before turning back to his duties.

"Well, I never," said Aurora. "He didn't have to be so rude."

"He was just doing his job," said Theo, keeping his hand on Aurora's shoulder to guide her along. "When people come in here for the first time, they naturally stop and stare."

"Who says I haven't been here before?" she asked. "I'll have you know, my girlfriends and I had lunch in the Oak Room just last week."

"Don't get your dander up." Theo chuckled. "If you've been here before, then you know that young ladies aren't allowed in the Oak Room without an escort. And they don't serve lunch."

Ladies needed an escort? What kind of place was Theo taking her to? Then she saw the entrance.

Where the Plaza Hotel's lobby was all about splendor and light, the Oak Room was a hideaway of shadows and secrets. Beyond the thick wooden doors, Theo led her through a winding passage paneled in knotted oak, duskily lit with low-hanging lamps. The faces of the patrons were masked in a haze of cigarette smoke as they drew closer together in their private conversations.

Aurora had never been in this kind of establishment before. She shuddered to think how she would explain it to her parents if she had to. But she couldn't turn around and leave, not with the boys waiting for her.

"Bill tipped the waiter and got us a brilliant table," said Theo, pointing to the far side of the room. It was the only bright spot in the lounge, with windows overlooking the south lawn of Central Park. Bill and Eddie were already seated, talking with one of the servers.

"Oh, and here's the rest of our group now." Bill waved them over. "I was just ordering. They make a divine Bloody Mary in beef bouillon with a shrimp garnish. I highly recommend it."

Eddie shook his head. "No fancy drinks for me. I'll have a beer."

"Coffee, black," said Theo, pulling a deep leather chair out from the table for Aurora.

"Something for you, miss?" asked the waiter.

Aurora took her seat. She hadn't the faintest idea what to order. The only alcohol she'd ever tried was the eggnog Mother served on New Year's Eve, and she didn't like the bitter taste of coffee.

"She'll have a Pink Lady," said Theo. "And make it for a proper young lady," he added.

"Excellent choice," said Bill.

"Very well, sir." The waiter jotted down a few marks on his note pad. "I'll be back with your orders, gentlemen. And yours, miss." He nodded toward Aurora before leaving.

"What's a Pink Lady?" she asked, almost afraid to hear the answer.

"You'll love it," said Bill. "Just right for a sweet young lass like you."

Although they were only a few years older than her, Aurora felt like a child seated at the table for the grown-ups. Bill and Eddie were dressed in tailored, vested suits, with high, starched collars and bow ties. Eddie's hair was still barely combed, but Bill's was slicked down with a tonic to make his meticulous part.

Even Theo had traded in his old gray sweater and blue slacks for a pinstripe jacket and matching trousers. He looked downright handsome, all clean-shaven and dressed to the nines. He could have been sitting with the cosmopolitan girl out in the Palm Court instead of here with Aurora, in her schoolgirl woolens and clunky leather boots.

"Take your coat off, Aurora," said Bill. "Make yourself comfortable."

"Yeah, what's the matter?" asked Eddie. "You look like you don't recognize us."

Aurora undid a couple buttons but left her coat on. She didn't plan to stay long.

"It's just that you look so different from how I usually see you over at the academy," she said. "I mean, you hardly seem like the same boys."

"You don't think we run around in pirate costumes and greasepaint all day, do you?" asked Bill.

"Although Eddie here would much rather be in his dungarees and baseball cap," said Theo.

"Ah, cut it out," said Eddie.

"Do you boys come to the Plaza often?" asked Aurora.

"Often?" Bill let out a hearty laugh. "Theo lives on the fourteenth floor. His family's practically got the whole wing."

Theo shook his head.

"It's not that grand," he said. "It's mainly just me and the maid in a couple of rooms. My parents spend most of their time in Europe."

"You should see the views of the city from up there," said Bill. "And Theo can look down into the windows of the Vanderbilt's dining room and tell you what they're having for dinner."

"My goodness," said Aurora. Who would have thought unassuming Theo Eckstein was from a family that could afford living full-time in the Plaza Hotel?

"It's a lot different from my family's apartment," said Eddie. "Six of us crammed into two rooms on the Lower East Side."

"Eddie came over from Romania," Theo explained to Aurora, "when he was just ten years old."

"My goodness," Aurora said again. Each of these boys had a story to tell.

"Even your name was different back then, wasn't it, Eddie?" asked Bill. "Emanuel Goldenberg, or something like that?"

"Yeah, the dean of the drama school told me I should change it," he said. "To make me sound more American."

"But why did you have to pick something so long?" asked Bill. "Edward G. Robinson. No one's going to remember that when you start going for auditions."

"Like William Powell is ever going to stick in their minds." Eddie countered. "Sounds as boring as that little town you came from."

"Watch what you're saying." Bill rose to the challenge. "I'll have you know the joints in Kansas City are as tough as any in the Bowery."

"Aw, come on. You haven't seen tough."

"Fellas, put a lid on it." Theo cut in. "Remember, we asked Aurora to come here to tell us what she knows about the professor. We haven't even given her a chance to talk yet."

Three sets of eyes turned her way, but Aurora wished the boys would continue on with their squabbling. Despite all her thinking this afternoon, she hadn't come up with any clues about Professor Schmieder. Well, except for one little detail that could hardly amount to anything.

"Go on," said Theo, softening his voice. "You did think of something, didn't you?"

Bill and Eddie leaned in closer.

"It's probably nothing," she said.

"Let us be the judge," said Bill. "You spent time with him every week. Did he seem different to you lately?"

"No, nothing like that." She hesitated. "You're going to think I'm being foolish."

"We won't," said Theo. "Go ahead."

"It's just that I was thinking today about how he seemed so proper and old-fashioned in everything he said and did. You know, you saw him. His clothes, the furniture in his studio. Even the music he had me working on. He hated all modern music. You should have heard him complain about Sibelius, and those symphonies by Maestro Mahler."

"I can't make it through one of Mahler's concerts, either," said Bill. "Two hours of just sitting there, listening to the orchestra rumble along without a tune you can whistle after the show."

"Bill." Theo looked in his direction. "Aurora's talking."

She took a breath and began again.

"Anyway, every once in a while during my lesson, he would start playing a popular song on the piano just to fill the time. It always struck me as odd. I mean, why would he know a tune from Tin Pan Alley?"

Theo nodded knowingly at Bill and Eddie.

"See, I told you," he said.

"What?" asked Aurora.

"Did you hear that violinist playing in the Palm Court before you came in?" asked Bill.

"Of course, that's why I was late in meeting you. I was feeling sorry for him because nobody else was paying attention."

"Your violin teacher used to have that job on Sunday afternoons," said Theo. "Playing all the requests for the ladies' teatime crowd."

"Professor Schmieder?" asked Aurora. "You must be joking. He was classically trained in a music conservatory."

"I saw him playing there a few weeks ago," said Theo. "I was going to introduce myself and tell him I recognized him from the Carnegie Towers. But he packed up his violin and left as soon as he played his last number. Like he was ashamed to be there."

"I don't understand," said Aurora. "Surely he didn't need the money." After all, Mother was always complaining about the cost of her lessons, even though Grandmother paid for them.

"Maybe he didn't have enough students," said Eddie. "You're the only one we ever saw go in there. Except for the lady this morning."

It seemed so long ago, but Aurora did remember the boys mentioning another student coming in before her.

"Ah, yes," said Bill, gazing into the distance. "She was a vision of loveliness stepping off the elevator, in her violet traveling gown and gorgeous mink wrap."

"To be honest, we didn't exactly see her face because of the veil she was wearing," said Eddie. "But from what we could tell, she was a real dame. Didn't you think so, Theo?"

"The only thing I noticed was that she wasn't carrying a violin," he said.

Good old Theo, thought Aurora. *Always the practical one.*

"You know, that was funny," said Bill. "She walked down the hallway and knocked on the professor's door. They talked for a few seconds, and then he let her in."

"Didn't you see her when she came out?" asked Aurora.

"Nah, she must have left while we were changing into our costumes," said Eddie. "The next beautiful gal we saw was you."

Aurora smiled at the compliment, but she was more interested in the mystery woman.

"I've never seen anyone like that around the professor's studio," she said. "He didn't seem to know many people."

"Maybe she was his daughter," said Eddie.

"Professor Schmieder wasn't married," said Aurora. "He told me he came to New York from Germany by himself. He played in the Philharmonic for a few years, and then he retired and started teaching."

"Did he talk to you much during your lessons?" asked Theo. "I mean, about his personal life?"

"Not really." She paused. "Except once, when I was telling him about how Grandmother and I like going to the Philharmonic concerts on Sunday afternoons. He said it must be nice to have family so close by."

"Finally." Bill was looking past Aurora. "Here comes our waiter. I thought he'd never get here. I'm as dry as the Sahara."

The server set their orders on the table. Aurora's was a frosted glass filled with a frothy pink liquid and topped off with a bright-red maraschino cherry. It looked so pretty that she didn't want to drink it.

Bill and Eddie were less inclined to ponder the looks of their refreshments, taking long gulps to quench their thirsts. On their faces, she could see sly grins emerging. Oh dear, they were going to get tipsy right in front of her, in the middle of the afternoon.

"Go ahead, Aurora. Try yours," said Bill, before popping the shrimp garnish into his mouth.

"I don't know," said Aurora. Still, Theo had gone to the trouble of ordering it for her. She took the glass and brushed the foam against her lips. Hmm, tasted nice.

"Isn't it sweet?" asked Theo. "Like I told you."

Aurora took a sip, and then a bit more. She had to admit, it was delicious.

"Theo, tell Aurora what else you found out about the professor," said Eddie, as they settled back in their chairs.

"I was talking to the manager of the Palm Court earlier this afternoon," said Theo. "I was telling him about the professor and that he'd have to find a replacement for him."

"No kidding," said Bill, although none of them were laughing.

"I know it's only been a few hours," said Aurora. "But it's hard to imagine the professor not being around, or to think about what happened to him."

"You're right," said Eddie. "I never much liked the guy, but that's still a rough way to go."

"That's why we're here," said Theo. "To try to figure out what really went on this morning." He took a sip of his coffee. "The Palm Court manager told me that Professor Schmieder was playing a couple of other gigs around town. Seems like he was accepting any and all offers. Even in a little cabaret off of Second Avenue."

"A cabaret?" asked Aurora. "You mean where they have dancing girls?"

"And a whole lot more," said Eddie, smiling like a Cheshire cat. "The place is in my neighborhood and a pal of mine runs it. Anytime we want to go over there, he'll get us great seats. Close to the stage so you can see everything."

With his hands, he outlined the figure of a shapely woman.

"Watch it, Eddie," said Theo. "We have a lady at our table."

Eddie mumbled something under his breath, but kept quiet.

"Hold on," said Bill. "We haven't even had a toast yet. To Aurora, for spending her afternoon with us."

"Hear, hear," said Theo, tipping his cup against Aurora's glass.

"Bottoms up, fellas," said Eddie. "Sorry, and lady."

He and Bill finished their drinks as Aurora took another sip of hers.

Uh-oh, she thought, slumping back in her chair. *I'm the one starting to get woozy.*

"Are you okay?" Theo took the glass from her hand and set it on the table.

"I'm fine," she said, but she didn't feel that way.

"Maybe you should take off your coat," said Bill. "Your face is kind of flushed."

"But all she had was syrup," said Eddie.

Theo signaled for him to be quiet.

"She'll be fine as soon as she gets outside," he said. "Besides, she needs to be home before O'Shea shows up."

Aurora winced. She'd forgotten about the detective.

"We should be going, too, fellas," said Theo. "I've got an idea."

Aurora wanted to ask him what he was thinking about, but as she pushed her seat back from the table, she clumsily got her coat tangled up in the chair leg. Couldn't she do anything right?

"Wait a minute," said Theo. "Let me help you."

And Aurora knew that he would.

Chapter 6

THE GRANDFATHER CLOCK WAS beginning its solemn announcement of four chimes when Aurora ducked into the apartment.

Whew, back on time. Glancing at herself in the hall mirror, she could hardly believe she had just been sitting in the fancy Plaza Hotel with three good-looking young men. Just like grown-ups in their own real-life drama, complete with the professor as the unfortunate victim, Aurora as the unjustly accused heroine, and Bill and Eddie as the two fleet-footed detectives. All acted out under Theo's watchful director's eye.

She cupped her hand over her mouth and blew into it. Good, there was only a tinge of sweetness from the Pink Lady on her breath. Now she had to check in on Grandmother, who was probably just starting to stir from her afternoon nap.

But instead of gentle snoring, she heard a deep voice coming from the sitting room. Was there a strange man in there with Grandmother? Aurora hurried down the hallway. Then as she got closer, the man's thick Irish accent started to sound familiar.

Suddenly, a woman's shrill voice rang out. A voice unmistakably known to her.

"Aurora Elizabeth! March right on in here, young lady!"

Aurora contemplated running in the other direction, but she knew that would only delay the inevitable. Taking a deep breath, she squared her shoulders and walked toward her destiny.

Mother and Father were seated on the low couch in the parlor, still wearing their coats and looking sterner than she'd ever seen them. The reason for her parents' consternation was seated across the coffee table from them, Detective Barney O'Shea. Wasn't he supposed to be here *after* four? The detective's large frame filled the already crowded room, as he perched precariously on a spindly-legged footstool with his coat folded over his arms. He must have gotten there even before her parents, but who let him in?

Aurora turned to the corner of the room. Grandmother was just where she had left her, awake but with a rather sleepy-looking smile on her face. Her hands were neatly folded in her lap. On the table to her side was her favorite tea setting. But next to the teapot there was a bottle of liqueur Mother took out only on special occasions. Uncorked and half empty.

"Aurora Elizabeth."

Aurora's heart sank. Her father never called her by her full name.

"We left you here to take care of your grandmother," he said.

"Now look at her." Mother chimed in. "She emptied the liquor cabinet and was playing the Victrola loud enough to frighten the neighbors. I don't know what would have happened if this nice policeman hadn't stopped by."

"Detective, ma'am. Detective O'Shea."

Mother took no notice.

"Who knows what else your grandmother might have done?" she said. "Gone traipsing out into the street in her slippers, or some such nonsense."

"For heaven's sake, Marguerite," said Father. "Mother was just enjoying listening to the opera. Although how she figured out how to turn on the player, I don't know."

Aurora stole a look back at Grandmother, who was nodding her head in quiet satisfaction.

"This nice detective knocked on the door," Mother went on. "And she let him in. But think if he might have been a thief." She gasped. "Or something worse. She just let him right into the apartment."

"I did show her my badge, Mrs. Lewis."

Aurora could tell the detective was starting to get impatient. Mother affected people that way.

"I asked if I could talk to you or your husband," said O'Shea. "And she said you'd be home soon and invited me in to wait. She even fixed me some of her special tea."

He pointed to the cup on the table in front of him.

"Then why is it that you want to talk with us?" asked Father.

Up to now, Aurora was only in trouble for leaving her grandmother alone. Wait until her parents heard why the detective was really here.

"You haven't told them yet?" O'Shea asked her.

"Told us what?" Mother arched her eyebrows, always a bad sign. "Aurora, what's this all about?"

The detective decided to take matters into his own hands.

"There was an incident at the Carnegie Towers today. Your daughter's violin teacher had an accident." O'Shea took a small notebook out from his shirt pocket to read from. "Professor Anton Schmieder."

"Aurora, why didn't you say something about this earlier?" asked Mother.

"I tried to tell you."

"I didn't hear you say anything about it," said Mother. "Did you, Winston?"

"To be fair," said her father, "we barely gave Aurora a chance to say 'hello.' You were in such a hurry to get to your blessed brunch."

"Winston, please. I'm sure the officer isn't interested in our social calendar."

Detective O'Shea cleared his throat.

"As I was saying, your daughter's teacher had an unfortunate accident. Seems he lost his footing near an open window." He paused for a moment. "He didn't survive the fall."

The room was silent, but not for long.

"Oh my." Mother could always be counted on to fill the void. "How dreadful."

Aurora looked intently at the detective, wondering if she had heard him correctly. An accident? What about the boys in the alley, who said they had seen someone push Professor Schmieder out the window? Or to be more precise, that they had seen Aurora push him.

If the detective noticed her staring at him, he didn't show it. Instead, he placed the notebook back in his pocket and turned to her parents.

"Your daughter happened to come into the music studio just after the accident. Naturally she was quite upset, and I wanted to drop by and see how she was doing."

Mother stood up and drew Aurora close to her.

"You poor child. What a shock, and at such a young age."

Father was characteristically more analytical.

"You're saying Aurora's teacher fell out of a window? Why would he have the window open in the middle of winter?"

"Seems the heating system wasn't regulating properly in the studio, Mr. Lewis, and it was getting too warm in there for him."

Too warm? It had been freezing in the studio when she came in just a few minutes after the professor fell. Aurora squirmed out of her mother's embrace. Now the detective was looking at her.

"I suggest you keep a close eye on this young lady," said O'Shea. "She may be suffering from delayed shock, given what she saw today. We want to keep her safe."

This morning, Detective O'Shea had been all gruffness and business with Aurora. Why was he concerned with her well-being this afternoon?

"We will, officer." Mother assured him. "Thank you so much for coming over to check on her."

The detective rose to leave, taking care not to knock over the wobbly footstool or bump into the coffee table.

"Yes, thank you for your time," said Father, standing up and shaking the detective's hand. "I've always said how much I admire the good work the police department is doing in this city."

"It's just part of our job, sir," said Detective O'Shea. "You mind your parents now, Miss Lewis." He patted Aurora on the head. "Keep to your studies and stay out of trouble."

"She's a good girl, aren't you, dear?" Mother kissed her on the forehead.

The detective turned to Grandmother. "And thank you, ma'am. I don't know when I've had a better cup of tea."

Grandmother responded with a slight smile.

"I'll see you out." Father led the detective to the front door. As soon as they were beyond earshot, Mother dropped the doting maternal act.

"Aurora, I told you those violin lessons would lead to trouble. Spending your Saturdays with a half-crazed professor who didn't know well enough to keep from falling out a window." She wagged her finger at her. "Then a policeman comes by the house. What will the neighbors say?"

"Mother, please."

"And don't think I've forgotten about you leaving your grandmother alone this afternoon."

The woman had a steel trap for a mind, Aurora had to grant her that.

"Where did you go, anyway?" her mother asked. "Your hair smells of smoke, and your breath like cough syrup."

Darn, she had forgotten about the atmosphere of the Oak Room.

"Don't even bother making up another story," said Mother. "You're getting too cheeky for your own good. You know, Mirabelle Stevens has been telling me about a finishing school where she sends her daughter, Lucy. A place where you can learn how to become a proper young lady. They have classes in etiquette during the week, and on Saturdays they host teas for the girls and their mothers."

"But, Mother! You know how busy I am already, with my schoolwork and music lessons."

"Don't raise your voice at me, missy." Mother headed out of the parlor. "Besides, your music lessons are over. As for your behavior this afternoon, your father and I will have a talk about it. You're to stay in your room for the rest of the weekend."

Defeated, Aurora fell onto the couch and buried her head in her hands. What did it matter if the police no longer thought she was a suspect? She was already sentenced to a worse fate. Classes on manners and how to make pleasant conversation with prissy girls like Lucy Stevens. And those awful tea parties with her mother.

What about her master class with Maud Powell next Saturday, and her dream to be a professional violinist? Didn't she have anything to say about how her life was going to turn out?

"Aurora." A soft voice called to her. "Aurora, dear."

"Yes, Grandmother?" She raised her head.

"Come here, dear."

"What is it?" Aurora went over to her. "Can I get something for you?"

"Freshen up my tea, child. Before your mother locks away the spirits."

"Grandmother, you're full of surprises," said Aurora, pouring a dollop into the tea cup.

"Don't be stingy now." Grandmother patted her hand. "And about your mother, leave her to me."

"But what about the finishing school? You know how Mother is once she gets an idea."

"I still have something to say about how my granddaughter's trust fund is being spent. You keep up with your violin playing and make your grandmother proud."

Chapter 7

"HAVE YOU GOT THAT skeleton key on you, Eddie?" asked Theo, glancing down the empty hallway outside Professor Schmieder's studio.

Eddie held up a slender brass shank with a closed loop on one end and a flat, rectangular tooth on the other. "You know I always come prepared," he said. "Growing up in my part of town has its advantages, especially when it comes to being creative with the hardware."

"Then get us in there as quick you can," said Theo. "There's no telling if the police are going to be back again this afternoon or not."

"Give me a minute, why don't ya?" Eddie jiggled the bit in the door lock. "I don't do this kind of thing every day."

The boys heard a clanking noise at the end of the corridor and froze in place. But the elevator continued on its upward path, not bothering to stop at the fourth floor.

"That was close," said Theo.

Bill moved in for a better view of Eddie's fumblings.

"You sure you know how to use that thing?" he asked.

Eddie took a deep breath and didn't answer. Then with a determined flick of the wrist, the lock tumblers clicked into place and the door to the professor's studio opened.

Theo slipped in past Eddie, with Bill right on his heels.

"So much for a thank-you," said Eddie, quietly pulling the door shut after himself.

"Son of a gun," said Bill, surveying the room. "The police sure took this place apart." Sofa cushions were tossed upside down, sheet music dumped on the floor, even the shades on the table lamps were askew.

Theo whistled under his breath.

"Do you think they found what they were looking for?"

"What are we looking for?" asked Eddie.

"I don't know yet," said Theo. "Just keep your eyes open."

The young men fanned out across the room. The winter sun had already begun to set and the studio was nearly dark, but they didn't dare turn on a lamp for fear of drawing attention from any outside observers.

"Looks like the professor went to the symphony last night," said Bill, picking up a concert program lying on the piano. "Let's see what they were playing."

He turned to the inside pages.

"Ah, no wonder. There was a violin piece on the program. Only that's odd." He made sure he was reading the description correctly. "It says here the soloist was a lady named Maud Powell. When did they start letting women play with the orchestra?"

"There are only a few women who are professional musicians." Theo took the program from him. "Maud Powell is considered one of the pioneers. Schmieder must have been interested in her. See how he folded the corner of the page with her biography."

"Or maybe he was bored," said Bill. "I make paper airplanes when I can't stay awake during a concert."

Theo shrugged, dropping the program back onto the piano.

"Not much over here," said Eddie, rifling through the papers strewn across the parlor table. "A couple of laundry bills. A napkin from the Palm Court with some scribbles on the back."

"Take a look at what I found in the piano bench," said Bill, motioning for Theo to join him.

Using the scant light from the window, they paged through an album of sepia-toned photographs taken of a young man with flowing blond hair, dressed in a tuxedo and holding a violin under his chin in a Paganini pose.

"Do you think he's the professor?" asked Bill.

"Must be," said Theo. "These look like old studio pictures."

"Well, I'll be!" They heard Eddie exclaim but couldn't make out where he was in the shadows.

"What is it?" asked Theo.

"You should see this."

Theo and Bill followed Eddie's voice to a curtained-off space on the other side of the room.

"What are you doing in there?" asked Theo, drawing back the drapery.

Eddie was standing next to a low, narrow cot that barely fit into the cramped quarters. Two dark suits and a winter coat hung on a clothesline strung across the makeshift bedroom. A narrow window with a cracked pane allowed in a sliver of sunshine, along with the cold north wind. Cardboard boxes stacked underneath probably held the sum total of Professor Schmieder's personal effects.

"He must have been so down on his luck he couldn't afford rent on a separate apartment," said Theo.

"But where did he wash? In the men's room down the hall?" asked Bill. "Ugh."

"What's this?" asked Eddie, reaching down in between the cot and the wall.

He held up a left-handed red leather glove.

"That doesn't look like it belonged to the professor," said Bill.

Theo reached over to feel the leather between his thumb and forefinger.

"Check if there's a label inside," he said.

"If I can find it." Eddie turned the glove over for a better look. "Here it is. Feldman's Fine Leather."

"That's a shop down in Greenwich Village," said Theo. "My mother orders gloves for me from there every year for my birthday."

He didn't add that his parents were usually on vacation when his birthday came around, and he would receive the gloves in the store's plain brown box among the other gifts his mother never had time to wrap.

Eddie tried to fit the glove onto his own oversized mitt.

"Whoever wore this sure has small hands."

A moment later his face lit up.

"It's our lucky day." Eddie pulled out a tightly rolled bill from the forefinger of the glove. As he opened it, the bearded face of John Sherman looked up at him.

Eddie gasped. "It's a fifty. No, two fifties. One rolled up inside the other. Who would have left this much money lying around?" He paused. "Oh, wait a minute."

"What is it?" asked Bill.

"Never mind," said Eddie.

"Do you know who the glove belongs to?" asked Theo.

Eddie kept quiet.

"Speak up, Eddie," said Bill.

"You know, don't you?" asked Theo.

"Maybe," said Eddie. "It's just that when I saw Aurora this morning, she was wearing red gloves like these, and she does have small hands. I always wondered how she could get around on those violin strings."

Theo thought back to his walk home with Aurora earlier in the day. She had kept her hands in her coat pockets the whole way. He figured it was because he was carrying her violin. But if her hands were in her pockets because she'd lost a glove, that would be another story.

For the first time, Theo was obliged to consider what secrets Aurora Lewis might be hiding behind her schoolgirl charms. He didn't like what he was thinking.

"Give me the glove," he said. "And the money, too."

"Aw, why can't we have a little fun with it?" Eddie scowled, not wanting to relinquish his good fortune.

"Come on, Eddie," said Theo. "It doesn't belong to us."

Eddie slid the money back inside the glove and handed it over. But he was none too happy about it.

"Let's get out of here," said Theo. "I think we've seen enough."

Detective O'Shea stepped back into a darkened corner of the Carnegie Hall lobby, charting the course of the descending elevator car. From the fourth floor, it moved to the third and then the second.

He'd already gotten word from the precinct captain to close out the Schmieder case as an accident. No sense in spending police time trying to figure out why an old man fell from a window, not when there were real crimes out there waiting to be solved. But O'Shea was sure the professor didn't end up in the alley because of his own carelessness. That's why after meeting with the Lewis family he decided to take another look around Schmieder's studio, strictly off the record.

The elevator doors clanked open and three well-dressed young men stepped out. O'Shea tried to shrink himself into the corner even more, but it wasn't necessary. The fellows were too busy backslapping each other and laughing to pay any attention to their surroundings.

"Why don't we go up to Columbus Circle and see what's playing?"

That voice belonged to Theo Eckstein, the smart talker from the drama school.

"Great idea," said one of Eckstein's buddies. "I hear they've got a new act with six Albanian lady wrestlers."

"I'd rather see the show with Abdul and his harem of dancing wives," said the third. "Something more cultural."

What were the young men doing here late on a Saturday afternoon? If they were leaving after a play practice, where were the other students?

Detective O'Shea could have stopped them before they headed out the door. But he didn't want to let on that he was still looking into the Schmieder case and then have them tell the Lewis girl. Best to keep an eye on her without her knowing about it.

Still, it didn't sit well with him that he couldn't explain why the three young men were up on the fourth floor.

Chapter 8

SUNDAY MORNING CREPT INTO Sunday afternoon at the Lewis household. The temperature had dropped into the low teens overnight, prompting Mother to declare that God would understand if they didn't attend church today. They would instead spend their time at home considering their transgressions. Aurora couldn't help but notice Mother's icy stare during their breakfast prayers. As for Father, as soon as the dishes were cleared, he was out the door and off to his club. Cold weather made little difference to him when there was an opportunity to escape both the minister's and his wife's lecturing on a Sunday.

Aurora spent the rest of her morning sulking in the bath. Usually she pretended she was a royal princess, luxuriously soaking in the deep-clawed tub surrounded by rose garlands etched into the bathroom tile. But today she resigned herself to scrubbing every inch of her scalp to get rid of the cigarette smell from the Oak Room. After rinsing, she combed out the tangles one by one. No point in hurrying. There wouldn't be any change in Mother's verdict of house confinement for the rest of the weekend, including missing Maud Powell's performance with the Philharmonic this afternoon.

Padding down the hallway in her sheepskin slippers, she noticed Grandmother hadn't made it out of her bedroom yet. Although neither of her parents said anything at dinner last night, Aurora guessed that Grandmother was nursing a headache after her own escapades yesterday. The only sign of life was the half-empty glass of tomato juice outside her door, which Father must have brought her before making his getaway.

Back in her room, the cheerful daisy wallpaper and pink embroidered pillowcases only served to further dampen Aurora's mood. Seeing the framed photograph of Miss Powell on her dresser, welcoming her as a new member of the Maud Powell Society, depressed her all the more. Even her collection of China dolls, with their inscrutable smiles, seemed to be enjoying her misery.

Aurora climbed back in under the bed covers. Shedding a few more well-deserved tears for herself, she could only ask, "What else can go wrong?"

First, there would be no more music lessons, despite her grandmother's assurances. When Mother set her mind on something, she was loathe to change it. Aurora had already stuffed her violin case into her closet, and she knew when her name was announced at Miss Powell's master class next Saturday, she wouldn't be on the stage to answer. She never even had the chance to tell Professor Schmieder she had been selected to perform.

Oh, that ill-fated lesson. If she'd only arrived at the studio a few minutes earlier, instead of joking with Theo and the boys, she might have been able to help the professor. Or at least she could have seen what really happened. Aurora didn't believe for a second that Professor Schmieder fell out of the window of his own accord, and she didn't think Detective O'Shea did either. So why the big act in front of her and her parents?

But what could she do, trapped in a bedroom decorated more for a little girl than a young woman nearly ready to graduate from high school? Could Mother be right about it being time she started acting her age?

Aurora covered her head with her pillow, appalled to think she was agreeing with her mother. Maybe it would all go away if she lay here forever, or at least until the bad news could be forgotten.

Warm and snug, with the steam radiator humming happily, Aurora let herself slip away.

Until someone gently started nudging her shoulder.

"Aurora. Aurora."

She pretended she was asleep.

"Child, are you ill?"

Aurora turned her head. Grandmother's soft brown eyes were looking down on her.

"Aurora, dear. Tell Grandmother if you're not feeling well."

"I'm fine." She rubbed her eyes. "What time is it?"

Then she saw that Grandmother's white hair was nicely styled, and she was wearing the ruby earrings she took out only for special occasions.

"Have you forgotten?" Grandmother's concerned expression began to soften. "We're going to the Philharmonic concert and you're not dressed yet."

The painful memory was starting to come back.

"But I can't," said Aurora. "You heard what Mother said."

"Dearest, now put on the new blue suit I bought you for Christmas. The one with the white piping. And don't forget your woolens, it's cold out there."

She touched Aurora's hair, which had dried into thick clumps.

"You'll have to pull this back into a bun and wear a hat. Your mother will never let us out of the house with you looking like a ragamuffin."

"How did you ever get her to change her mind?" asked Aurora, but Grandmother was already on her way out of the room.

"Hurry along, child," she said. "I don't walk as fast as I used to, and I've heard Maestro Mahler doesn't suffer latecomers."

Chapter 9

THROUGH THE THIN WALLS of her dressing room, Maud Powell could hear the Philharmonic's French horns launch into the opening calls of Wagner's *Flying Dutchman Overture*. She looked at herself in the mirror, pinning a few errant strands of her dark brown hair back into place. Her face, still youthful despite her forty-three years, was eager with anticipation. This afternoon's performance of the Beethoven concerto would be one to remember.

Maestro Mahler likes to keep the tempo moving in the first movement, she reminded herself, *and be sure to watch him during the transitions in the slow movement. Other than that, you're on your own.*

During her brief rehearsal time with the orchestra, the only communications she'd received from the conductor had been a couple nods on her entrances and an instruction for her to accent the downbeats more at the beginning of the *Rondo*. After a brisk run-through of the piece, Maestro Mahler was off the stage without another word, with a white silk towel wrapped around his neck and his assistant by his side.

No doubt Mahler's struggles with the Philharmonic's board of directors were taking their toll. Audiences were complaining about his penchant for programming modern music, including many of his own compositions, while the symphony musicians were grumbling about his frequent outbursts on the podium.

Yet after seeing Maestro Mahler clutch at his chest during last night's concert, Maud could sympathize a little with the generally unsympathetic conductor. Having experienced her own health problems, she knew the toll that concert pressures could take on a person.

A knock on the door interrupted her thoughts.

"Godfrey, is that you?" she called out.

"No, Miss Powell." The door opened to reveal the pencil-thin stage manager. "Just wanted to let you know you've got about ten minutes."

"Thank you," she said, smiling sweetly. "I'll be out shortly."

Maud's pleasant countenance faded as soon as the door closed. Where was her husband, Godfrey, anyway? Probably getting some work done at the office, even if it was a Sunday. As her manager, he was always on the lookout for her next engagement. His ingenuity in filling her schedule had stretched this concert set with the Philharmonic into an extended stay in the city, including a recording session on Wednesday, lecture on Thursday, and master class on Saturday. When all she really wanted to do was go home to their lovely house on Long Island.

But now wasn't the time to be sentimental. Maud took up her violin and stroked the finely grained wood. At least her old friend, Guadagnini, was here with her. Delicate to the touch, yet resilient enough to have created more than a century of music before coming into her most fortunate possession.

She positioned the violin under her chin and then took her bow in her right hand. She was softly playing through the arpeggios from the concerto's first movement cadenza when she heard another knock on the door.

"I said I'd be right out."

This time, her tone wasn't so friendly.

"Miss Powell, could I speak with you?"

That didn't sound like the meek stage manager.

"Miss Powell, it'll only take a minute." The man's voice was deep, with a strong Irish accent. "May I come in?"

He was probably an admirer wanting her autograph. But weren't the stage hands supposed to keep her fans away until after she played?

Maud took one more look in the mirror and smoothed out the bodice of her gold-laced evening gown. The wayward strand of hair had fallen out of place again, but she didn't have time to fix it.

"Just a minute," she called out.

Cradling her violin under her arm, she opened the dressing room door. Blocking her way was a large gentleman holding a concert program.

"Excuse me," she said. "But you'll have to wait until intermission for me to sign that."

The orchestra was already into the rousing finale of the overture.

"My concerto is coming up next on the program," she said.

The man didn't budge.

"Really, sir." She tried to walk by him. "I have to get to the stage."

"Then I'll go with you." He pulled out a shiny badge from his breast pocket. "Detective Barney O'Shea. From the New York City Police Department."

She halted in midstep.

"Let's move along, ma'am." He put his badge back into his pocket. "I don't want the conductor to get angry with me for making you late. I hear he has a fierce temper."

Maud walked toward the stage as quickly as her fitted gown would allow.

"Are you sure you have the right person, Detective?" she asked. "What could you possibly want to talk to me about?"

"It's about this concert program I found."

He held it up for her to see.

"What's so special about that?" asked Maud. "Those are printed up for every performance."

"This one was from your concert on Friday night," said Detective O'Shea. "But that's not why I'm interested in it."

"Detective, I don't understand what you're saying."

She turned the corner and headed for the stage door. To her dismay, the policeman kept pace with her.

"This program was found in a music studio next door, in the Carnegie Towers."

"I still don't understand."

"There was an accident over there yesterday morning. A teacher fell out of a window."

Maud kept on walking.

"When I searched his studio, I found this concert program," said the detective. "The page with your biography was folded over."

The waiting area for the stage was a small space to begin with, and the detective's wide girth took up most of it.

"I thought you might have heard about the accident," said O'Shea. "Or you might have known the teacher. He was an older gentleman."

"Detective, really."

The glorious B-flat major ending of the Wagner was ringing through the concert hall.

"There were nearly three thousand people at the concert on Friday night," she said. "Just because one of them was a violin teacher hardly means I know anything that might be of interest to you."

"Well, it was a long shot."

O'Shea stuffed the program into his coat pocket.

"I almost forgot to tell you. The teacher's name was Schmieder. Professor Anton Schmieder."

The audience was showering their approval onto the orchestra with loud applause. They did love their Romantic composers.

"I'm sorry." Maud pointed to her ear. "I didn't hear you."

The detective stepped in closer to her.

"His name was Anton Schmieder."

The stage door suddenly flew open toward them, sending the detective back a step. Moments later a short, wiry man wearing small, round spectacles charged off the stage, loosening his tie and pointing to his reddened face. From behind Detective O'Shea, a man rushed forward carrying a glass of water and a white silk towel. After a quick gulp and wipe of his brow, Maestro Mahler was back in front of the crowd for his curtain call.

"Detective, we'll have to talk later," said Maud. "If the Maestro catches you back here when he comes out again, we'll both be in trouble."

She turned away, holding her violin up to her ear to check the tuning. Out of the corner of her eye, she saw the detective linger for a few seconds and then take his leave.

The porridge-faced policeman was smarter than he looked, but all he had connecting her to Anton Schmieder was a concert program and a hunch. Maud took a deep breath and prepared to walk on stage. During the performance, she would forget the detective's untimely visit. And afterward, the audience's applause would all be for her.

O'Shea didn't need to wait around until after Miss Powell played. He was more partial to Irving Berlin than Beethoven, anyway. A couple of years moonlighting security at Carnegie Hall had taught him that much.

Besides, Maud Powell had told him everything he needed to know, from her nonanswers to her assumption that the departed professor was a violin teacher. She knew old Anton, maybe even knew him well. With that as a start, he would make some inquiries at the Algonquin Hotel. That's where the Philharmonic put up their guest musicians when they were in town, another bit of information he'd learned while working security on the classical music circuit.

But first he would drop by the Plaza Hotel to catch the last of the teatime program at the Palm Court. Rummaging around in the professor's studio yesterday, he'd happened upon a napkin from the restaurant, with a list of songs scribbled on the back. Somebody there might be able to tell him more about the professor. If not, at least he could order a nice cup of tea. Although probably not as tasty as Grandma Lewis's special recipe.

Chapter 10

THE LAST STRAINS OF Miss Powell's encore had barely faded away before Aurora was out of her seat, up the aisle, down two flights of stairs, across the lobby, and through the side door that led to the concert hall's backstage. Holding a music program and her grandmother's pen, she had twenty minutes to reach Miss Powell's dressing room, introduce herself, ask for her autograph, and then make it back up to the balcony in time for the second half of the concert.

She dodged by the tuxedoed musicians filling the backstage area. If Aurora hadn't been in such a hurry, she might have felt awkward being the only young lady in a sea of men. But for the most part they paid no attention to her, except for when one of the violin players noticed she looked lost.

"She's that way," he said, pointing toward a narrow corridor leading from the stage.

Aurora headed down the hallway at full speed, until she turned the corner and ran into a long line of admirers already waiting to see the afternoon's star performer.

Good grief. Aurora started counting the people ahead of her and gave up at fifteen. Looking at her watch, she realized she would either have to skip meeting Miss Powell, or wait for a pause between movements during the second half to sneak back to her seat. Aurora checked her program to see what the orchestra was playing after intermission and moaned so loudly that the lady standing in front of her turned around to see what was the matter.

The only piece left on the program was the Fourth Symphony composed by Gustav Mahler. Everyone knew Maestro Mahler loved writing long first movements, and sometimes the orchestra didn't even take a break before the second. Aurora could miss the rest of the concert altogether.

Darn it. Who were these people anyway, and how did they get here so quickly? They must have been sitting on the main floor, in the seats reserved for season ticket holders. Mainly women who probably didn't know anything about music but just wanted to say they had met someone famous like Maud Powell.

Aurora stood on her tiptoes to see if the line was moving. To her surprise, Theo was standing near the front of the queue, and he was waving for her to come forward.

She looked around, not wanting to upset the other autograph seekers by cutting ahead. But they seemed too absorbed in their conversations to pay attention. She looked again at Theo, who was beckoning her more urgently to join him.

As inconspicuously as she could, Aurora dashed to his side.

"Here." He slipped her into the line ahead of him. "I saved a spot for you."

The woman standing behind them was about to tap Aurora on the shoulder when Theo turned around to talk to her.

"Don't worry." He stepped to the side. "This young lady is a very fine violinist. I was just holding her place for her."

The woman glared at them for a moment, but when her companion started talking about the new window displays at Bloomingdale's, Aurora was quickly forgotten.

"How did you know I would be here?" she asked Theo.

"You told us that you and your grandmother like coming to the Sunday concerts."

Aurora was puzzled.

"When we were over at the Oak Room," he said.

"Oh, right," she said, wondering how Theo could have such a good memory for detail.

"But I didn't say anything about coming backstage today," she said.

"I just guessed on that one. I couldn't imagine you not wanting to meet Miss Powell in person."

He did seem to be able to read her mind.

"What did you think of her performance?" he asked.

Aurora hesitated before answering. There was a passage in the first movement where Miss Powell's tuning was slightly off, and she seemed to bobble an entrance in the *Rondo*. But she wasn't going to say anything negative about her favorite violinist.

"I thought she was wonderful," said Aurora. "Just wonderful."

"Hmm," said Theo. "I thought she seemed a little distracted. She kept shaking her head, like she was trying to get the hair out of her eyes."

Hmm. From where she and Grandmother were sitting in the upper balcony, they could barely see Miss Powell's face.

"Do you come to the Philharmonic often?" she asked.

"My parents have season tickets," said Theo. "When they're not in town, I can use them."

"That's nice," said Aurora. She and Grandmother had waited in the cold to buy their tickets.

"I did like Miss Powell's encore piece, though," said Theo. "Do you know what she played? It wasn't listed in the program."

"Do I know it?" said Aurora. "It's the same piece I'm playing—I mean, I was supposed to play at her master class. The Paganini 'Romanze.'"

The line shuffled ahead a few inches.

"What do you mean, you were supposed to play?" asked Theo.

"Let's just say my mother is determined to ruin my life," said Aurora. "After that visit from Detective O'Shea yesterday."

"You'll have to tell me later," said Theo. "I think you're next."

Aurora leaned forward to take a peek. There was the sleeve of a shimmering gold evening gown. Then she could see Miss Powell's face.

"It's really her." Aurora clapped her hands.

Theo grinned.

"I'll leave you now," he said, but Aurora barely heard him. Her focus was all on Maud Powell, who was only a few steps away.

"I'll wait for you in the lobby," said Theo.

Aurora nodded, but she was more concerned about making sure she had her program opened to the right place for Miss Powell to sign, right under her biography.

Now that she was ready she looked around for Theo, but he'd already left. For a moment, Aurora felt bad that she hadn't paid more attention to him. After all, he did save the place in line for her. She would apologize later, but since she was waiting, she could at least read about Miss Powell in the concert notes.

The biography started with a recounting of Maud Powell's first meeting with Maestro Theodore Thomas, who became her musical mentor and most influential supporter. Then the story shifted to Miss Powell's current busy schedule, which was managed by her husband, Godfrey Turner—Miss Powell used her maiden name as her stage name. But Aurora was most interested in Miss Powell's life as a girl growing up in Illinois, taking piano and violin lessons, and winning local music contests. In her teenage years, she moved to New York to focus on her violin studies, and then she completed her training in Europe.

Professor Schmieder used to tell Aurora that if she was really serious about becoming a musician, she had to live in Europe for at least part of her life. To walk in the footsteps of Mozart and hear the wandering brook of Schubert.

Aurora continued reading. Miss Powell studied in Heidelberg when she was in Europe. Now wasn't that a coincidence? Heidelberg was the town where the professor used to teach.

Theo took his time walking past the orchestra musicians milling around backstage during the concert's intermission. Among the violists, the small talk centered on the prospects for the New York Giants' upcoming season. The trumpet section traded jokes that would have made the gray-haired audience members blush, while the clarinetists lamented the effects of the frigid weather on their reeds.

But leave it to the violinists to be the gossips of the orchestra, and with Maud Powell as their guest artist, the comments were flowing freely.

"Did you hear her phrasing in the slow movement? I thought I was going to nod off."

"She has such a small sound, we had to play *pianissimo* the whole time to keep from drowning her out."

Then there were the players who found Miss Powell's personal life more interesting than her performance.

"She and the old man had a terrible row here on Friday night. You could hear them shouting through the dressing room walls."

Theo lingered by this group a little longer.

"Who was he, anyway?" asked someone else. "He looked familiar."

"Didn't you recognize him? That was Anton Schmieder. He was fired from the orchestra a couple years ago."

"My God. He's aged ten years since I last saw him."

"I heard Mahler finally got fed up with him missing too many rehearsals. Something about him having a problem with playing the horses."

"Sounds like he had a problem with the ladies, too." One of the violinists snickered. "From the way he and old Maudie were going at it."

Theo shook his head as he walked away. The musicians must not have heard the news about the professor's accident. When they did, they might feel sorry for how they had spoken about their former colleague.

Miss Powell took the pen and program from Aurora.

"What's your name, dear?"

Up close, she was even lovelier than Aurora had imagined, in a fragile sort of way. Her skin was pale and her smile taut, almost strained, as if she was making an effort to appear cheerful.

She was also smaller than Aurora expected. The stage must have added to her statuesque appearance during the performance. But standing next to Miss Powell, Aurora was the one looking down on her.

"My name is Aurora Lewis. I'm one of your biggest fans."

She suddenly felt out of breath.

"I've been a member of the Maud Powell Society since I was twelve. It's so exciting to meet you. My grandmother and I bought tickets to this concert weeks ago."

"Now isn't that nice, Anna."

Miss Powell started to sign the cover of the program.

"My name's Aurora. And if you don't mind signing here." She reached over to turn the page back to her biography in the program.

Miss Powell pursed her lips.

"I'm going to be in your master class next Saturday," said Aurora. "Here at Carnegie Hall."

Miss Powell looked up, like she was seeing her for the first time.

"Why, that's wonderful, Aurora." Miss Powell emphasized her correct name. "I love working with young musicians like yourself, so full of enthusiasm and talent."

She began writing "To Aurora" in the program.

"What are you playing in the master class?"

"The Paganini 'Romanze.' The same piece you played for your encore."

Miss Powell sighed. "The Paganini has some sad memories for me. But I still love to play it because it's such a beautiful piece."

"I think so, too," said Aurora. "And my music teacher said it was his favorite. That's why I chose it for the master class."

"Is that so?" Miss Powell finished writing the last two *ll*'s in her name with a flourish. "Who are you studying with?"

"Professor Schmieder." Aurora was thrilled that Miss Powell was spending so much time with her, although the fidgeting women standing in line weren't too happy about it.

"Schmieder?" repeated Miss Powell, handing back the signed program.

"Yes, he teaches next door." Then Aurora caught herself. "I mean, he taught next door, in the Carnegie Towers."

"That's very nice," said Miss Powell. Only now there was a hard edge in her voice, and the fake smile was back. "Enjoy the rest of the concert."

Before Aurora had a chance to thank her, Miss Powell had already turned her attention to the next gushing society lady. As she shuffled away, Aurora realized she had forgotten her grandmother's pen. But she couldn't go back and ask for it, not after Miss Powell had so abruptly brushed her aside.

She wandered by the symphony players as they waited to file back onstage for the concert's second half. As promised, Theo was waiting for her in the lobby.

"Why so glum?" he asked.

"I think she hates me." Aurora fought to hold back her tears.

"Why? What happened?"

"It was going so well." She showed him the autograph. "See what she wrote, 'To Aurora, with my best wishes.' We were talking about the master class, and then all of a sudden she practically pushed me out of the way to get to the next person."

"You're sure that's all you talked about?" asked Theo.

"I told her I was going to be playing the Paganini. Then she asked me who I was studying with."

She could feel the tears burning on her cheeks.

"On top of everything, I forgot Grandmother's pen," she said. "It was her best one, too."

Theo patted her on the shoulder.

"Don't cry, Aurora. I can help you get your grandmother another pen. And trust me, Maud Powell doesn't hate you. It's not about you at all."

"But you weren't there. You didn't see her."

"I'll explain what I mean," said Theo. "I also want to hear about what happened with Detective O'Shea yesterday. But first, there's something I need to know."

When Theo Eckstein asked her about the red glove during the intermission of the Philharmonic concert, Aurora thought he was joking. Didn't he realize she had a dead professor, a curious policeman, an irate mother, and an angry Miss Powell to worry about?

"What a silly question, Theo. It's in the pocket of my coat, along with my other glove. On my seat next to my grandmother."

"Are you sure?" he asked. "You wore them both here this afternoon?"

"Sure, I'm sure," she said. "It's freezing today. Do you want to climb up two flights of stairs so you can see for yourself?"

"Aurora, you can keep your voice down." Theo nodded to the patrons standing nearby who were watching the agitated young lady.

"It's just that I don't appreciate being talked to like I'm ten years old." Aurora lowered her voice to a whisper. "Why are you asking me this, anyway?"

Theo pulled out a red glove from his coat pocket.

"Me and the guys found this, and I wanted to make sure it's not yours."

Aurora took the glove. "Where did you find it?"

"Over in the Towers," said Theo.

"It's almost like mine." She touched the glove to her cheek. "It looks like it's made from the same leather."

She checked the inside label for the maker.

"It's from Feldman's, the same place Father bought my gloves. But look here."

She pointed to a small *M* monogrammed in black thread on the cuff.

"Whoever this belong to, her first name starts with *M*. The initial of her last name would be on the right-hand glove. Feldman's stitches that in for you if you ask them."

Theo took a closer look.

"I guess I didn't notice before," he said.

Aurora tried on the glove but had trouble fitting it over her knuckle.

"This must belong to someone who has even smaller hands than me."

Theo took a deep breath and relaxed.

"Here," she said, handing the glove back.

"No," he said. "You keep it."

"But why?"

One of the ushers walked by ringing a handbell, giving the two-minute warning for the end of intermission.

"It's getting late," said Aurora. "I should get back to Grandmother."

"I'll walk up with you." Theo took her by the arm. "I want to talk to you about doing something tomorrow. It concerns Maud Powell."

Chapter 11

THE CLOCK ABOVE THE blackboard must be running slow. Aurora was sure that when she last checked it was quarter till two. Now it was only fourteen minutes to the hour.

She scanned the faces of her classmates to see if they had noticed that time was standing still. Lucy Stevens, the teacher's pet, was sitting at the front of the room listening attentively to Miss Ferrier describe the life cycle of the tiger moth, as if it was the most fascinating subject in tenth grade. Sitting behind Aurora, Bobby Trenton was carving a curse word into the top of his school desk. And next to him, the class clown, Jimmy Childers, was pulling on the pigtails of Molly Monroe, the class flirt.

Thirteen minutes to freedom. Usually the days didn't drag on as long as this one. In the morning, Aurora giggled with her girlfriends before the school bell rang. Then she pretended to be interested in Miss Ferrier's lecture on Shakespeare and tried diligently to finish her mathematics problems.

Lunchtime gave Aurora a chance to sit with her friends and play one of their favorite games, rating the boys in the class on who would make the best husband, based on personality, good looks, and bonus points if they were already starting to show a mustache. Tony Silva won, of course, like he did every time. And true to his rascal nature, he cast the moonstruck girls a cocky smile when he walked out of the lunchroom, as if favoring them with his presence was enough reward for their obvious devotion.

Only today Aurora was quiet during the competition. True, Tony had everything you could ask for. His Italian eyes made the girls swoon, plus he was the best athlete in the class. But for the first time he didn't even come close to Aurora's notion of an ideal young man. She was thinking of someone more on the quiet side, not too full of himself. Tall, maybe wearing glasses.

She looked at the clock again. Ten minutes and counting.

"Girls and boys, you have a few minutes to start reading the next chapter in your biology text." Miss Ferrier droned on mercilessly. "I want everyone to come prepared tomorrow to participate in our class discussion on mollusks."

The teacher peered over the top of her thick glasses to make sure the students were really reading. But her nearsighted eyes were no match for the notes passing between the girls at lightning speed.

Emily started with a scribble to Martha.

Martha nodded yes and then handed the note off to Violet.

Violet agreed, passing the slip of paper to Aurora.

"Soda after school?" it read.

Aurora shook her head.

Emily, Martha, and Violet gasped.

"Miss Ferrier," said Lucy Stevens. "The girls are being noisy again. It's disrupting my reading."

Miss Ferrier sighed, but she didn't have time to reprimand them. The school bell rang, and Aurora and her friends were out of their seats and heading toward the cloakroom in the back of the class.

"What's going on, Aurora?" asked Violet, bundling up in her rabbit fur jacket and matching mittens. "Why won't you come have a soda with us?"

"I just can't today, that's all," said Aurora, hurrying to put on her coat.

"I know why Aurora isn't coming," said Martha. "Aurora has a boyfriend. Aurora has a boyfriend."

"What?" Emily's eyes opened wide. Lucy, who was standing nearby, stopped buttoning her coat and moved in closer to listen.

"That's just silly," said Aurora, feeling her face get red. "Mother needs me at home this afternoon."

"Come on, Aurora," said Violet. "Who is he?"

"Anyone we know?" asked Emily.

"My mother saw them together," said Martha. "Yesterday at the symphony concert, in the lobby during intermission. Isn't that right, Aurora?"

At first she thought she could deny the whole thing, but it was obvious that her friends, plus nosy Lucy, weren't going to let her get away without an explanation.

"He's just a boy I met at my music lessons." She didn't need to be too specific. "He was saying how much he liked the Beethoven concerto, and I said I did, too."

"Mother said he was nice-looking." Martha lowered her voice. "But very serious."

The girls laughed, except for Lucy, who was taking in every word. No doubt when Mrs. Stevens saw her mother at the lady's club meeting later this week, her new beau would be their first topic of conversation.

"I've got to get going." Aurora slung her book bag over her shoulder. "I'll see you all tomorrow."

"Say 'hello' to dreamboat for us," Emily called after her.

Aurora was down the school steps before she could hear any more of the girls' teasing. She'd been talking with Theo, but not about Beethoven or any other composer.

He'd asked her to make a trip downtown this afternoon. And if she didn't catch the streetcar on Fifty-Sixth Street by two thirty, she'd be too late.

Chapter 12

DETECTIVE O'SHEA HAD MANAGED to waste the last two hours of his shift in a halfhearted attempt to look busy, moving files from one side of his desk to the other. But the case he really wanted to work on was tucked away in the top drawer.

With the station captain off to another function with the mayor, he pulled out the closed Schmieder file and started reading through his notes again.

Nothing too out of place, really, except that the professor slept in the closet of his music studio. But with rents being so high these days, he'd seen stranger.

Aurora Lewis looked like a normal kid, living with an overbearing mother, mousy father, and spunky grandma who liked to take a nip in the afternoon. Aurora did well in school and in her music lessons. The only problem with her was that she was too curious for her own good.

The background check of the young actors came up pretty clean, too. Eddie Robinson's real name was Emanuel Goldenberg. His father was hardworking, and for the most part Eddie stayed out of trouble. The Eckstein kid lived with the family help in the Plaza Hotel while his parents traveled around the world spending the money his grandfather made in real estate. Not much on William Powell either, except that he carried a big tab at a few of the finer restaurants around town.

O'Shea turned the page to the professor's obituary clipped from the city newspaper. Sad day when you realize it takes just a couple of paragraphs to sum up a man's life.

Anton Schmieder was born in Germany fifty-two years ago, although to the detective he'd looked a good ten years older. He began playing the violin when he was five. Studied at the Heidelberg Conservatory and eventually became their violin professor. Moved to another town called Leipzig to play in their orchestra and then immigrated to the United States, where he played in the New York Philharmonic for a few years before retiring and opening his teaching studio.

Detective O'Shea's conversations with a couple of the musicians down at Carnegie Hall had added a little more color to Schmieder's early retirement. Something about him having lost his technique on the violin, along with the distraction of always being down a dollar at the racetrack.

The detective turned back to the death notice. Not much more to say about the guy. Had no survivors. Services to be private. In other words, Schmieder would be buried in the city cemetery along with the other poor folks who didn't have family or friends to claim their body.

Detective O'Shea closed the folder and set it on his desk. As far as he could tell, the professor wasn't anything special. Just a cranky old man who couldn't keep away from the gambling clubs and who had a bad sense of balance around windows.

Then why did the whole business stick in his craw? Call it a hunch, but until that stuck feeling went away, he'd keep on poking and prodding. The old man deserved at least that much.

Chapter 13

WHEN AURORA AGREED TO visit Feldman's glove shop in Greenwich Village, she didn't have a chance to tell Theo she hadn't ridden on a streetcar by herself. Or that she'd never been on a subway train that went underground, where you couldn't see anything familiar like buildings or trees. But Theo had an afternoon class so she was on her own, and she wasn't about to let a small thing like being scared to death stop her.

Her first task, however, before ever setting out on her journey, had been to come up with a reason for why she wouldn't be home right after school. She needed to think of an excuse that would divert Mother's attention and at the same time get back into her good graces. Since she and Grandmother had come home from the concert yesterday, Mother had barely spoken two words to either of them.

That's why at the breakfast table this morning, she had an announcement to make.

"Mother, I've been thinking about what you said, and I think you're right. The young ladies' finishing school would be just the thing for me."

Father dropped his fork into his eggs and Grandmother set down her cup of coffee to watch Aurora's performance. Mother, on the other hand, went on eating her toast as if she hadn't heard her.

"If you don't mind," said Aurora. "I'd like to go over there after school today. To introduce myself to the teachers and see what classes they're offering this session."

Mother daintily wiped the corner of her mouth with her napkin.

"I'm pleased to hear you're finally coming to your senses," she said. "Why don't I meet you at your school so we can walk over there together?"

Aurora hadn't expected that response. On Mondays, Mother was always at the beauty salon until late in the afternoon.

"That's awfully nice," said Aurora. "But I can't ask you to miss your hair appointment. You've got so many engagements this week, and I know how you like to look your best."

"It is time for a touch-up," said Mother, lightly patting her coiffure. "I've got the charity ball planning committee tomorrow and the museum luncheon on Thursday."

"I'll go down to the finishing school by myself and look around," said Aurora. "I can't wait to get started."

That last line was so over the top even Grandmother had to stifle a giggle. But if Mother noticed, she didn't let on. Her daughter was finally going to become a proper young lady, and that's what mattered.

Having secured a few hours for her after-school jaunt, the next step was to overcome her fears about traveling alone. The first part of the trip, riding on the streetcar, wouldn't be so bad. She had taken the trolley often enough with Mother. It was just a matter of watching the other people and doing what they did.

Waiting at the stop, Aurora tightly held a nickel in her hand. Plenty of times Mother had boarded without giving a thought to the fare, creating a dustup with the conductor while she fumbled through her purse looking for a few loose coins.

The clanging bell alerted Aurora and her fellow travelers that their ride was on its way. As the tired horses pulled the car to the curb, she felt sorry for adding to the animals' burden but went ahead and found a seat near the front. Taking a quick look around, she was relieved she didn't recognize anyone. Wouldn't it be just her luck if one of Mother's friends sat down beside her, full of questions about where she was going all by herself on a school day?

"Your fare, miss." The uniformed conductor balanced himself on the streetcar's bottom step as it began to move forward.

Aurora dropped the nickel into his chapped hands. "Thank you, sir."

The man muttered something under his breath and then handed her a ticket and continued on to the next passenger. No matter if he was ill-tempered, Aurora was terribly pleased with herself for getting this far.

As the streetcar rumbled down the street, she silently repeated Theo's instructions. Get off at the fifth stop, at the intersection of Broadway and Forty-Second Street, where the new Coca-Cola building was being built. If she needed a landmark, a twenty-four story white skyscraper should do it.

But the streetcar kept getting more and more crowded as they traveled southward. Soon her view was completely blocked by a couple of strapping young men who were hanging on to the side for a free ride until the conductor made it back through the car. Aurora carefully counted the stops using her fingers, until she reached her pinkie.

"Excuse me, I have to get off," she said, trying to squeeze past the two fellows. But her soft voice was drowned out by the street noise.

"Excuse me," she said louder. "This is my stop."

The young men paid her no mind.

"I have to get off," she shouted, trying to move them out of her way. Finally they stepped aside to let her through, but her forward momentum flung her off the streetcar in an unintended leap. Her right foot landed in a pothole full of mud, and she was about to fall flat on her face when the streetcar conductor grabbed her by the collar and pulled her back from certain doom.

"Whoa there, little lady," he said. "You okay?"

Aurora stepped onto the sidewalk and tried to steady her shaking legs. After making sure she was still holding her book bag, she nodded that she was all right.

"Be careful, young lady." The conductor climbed back on board and rang the bell for the car to start moving again. Aurora glanced down the street, watching the two men who had been the cause of all her problems running away, with the conductor yelling at them to stay off his route.

Dazed for a minute, Aurora didn't see the Coca-Cola building until she nearly ran into the fencing surrounding the work site. The structure was so tall she couldn't even see the top floor from where she stood on the sidewalk. But she could tell that construction was going on from the shrill whistles and hammers banging above her. At least she was in the right place, and none the worse for wear except for the inch of mud on her winter boots.

With the first part of her trip complete, she saw a cavernous opening in the sidewalk up ahead. Watching people descend into the darkness, Aurora braced herself for the next leg of her adventure—the New York City subway.

The rush of acrid air was the first shock to her senses, as if the tunnel was belching out all the smoke and fumes it had accumulated during the day. She expected her fellow New Yorkers to notice the pungent smell, too. But they just brushed past her, stern-faced and in a hurry to get to whatever awaited them at the bottom of the concrete staircase. Aurora held on to the iron handrail and followed their lead.

Her next discovery was that there was a whole other city bustling underneath the avenue. Absent sunshine or nightfall, the alter metropolis revolved around its own schedule, timed with the coming and going of the trains. Tiny shop stalls survived on the flurry of passengers wanting to get a shoeshine, fill out a racing sheet, or grab a pizza slice before catching their ride.

Like the drab gray walls around them, the complexions of the shopkeepers were a sallow, unhealthy color. One motioned for her to come closer to try on a pretty scarf, but most figured that a schoolgirl wasn't going to have any extra money to throw their way and didn't give her a second look.

Which was fine with Aurora. Theo's directions were to take the "E" line to Greenwich, so she focused on reading the signs leading her deeper into the station. She reached into her pocket to pull out her second nickel of the trip. Lucky she hadn't spent all of this month's allowance on candy and hair ribbons. In Mother's current mood, there was no telling when she'd see another fifteen cents come her way.

At the ticket counter, she slid the nickel through the steel bars and waited. The subway agent slid over a larger coin in return. Aurora looked at it but didn't pick it up. Why was she getting money back?

"Take the token and move along," said the man, waving her toward the gates.

Aurora picked up the coin and stepped to the side. Like with everything else today, she copied the person in front of her, putting the token in the slot and then pushing the turnstile bars to enter.

But that was just the beginning. She still had to descend two more flights of steep stairs and walk the length of a long cement platform. If she had any misgivings about being trapped in an underground tunnel with hundreds of strangers, she was too far along to turn back now.

Then she had another moment of panic. She knew she was going south to Greenwich, but the signs didn't say which direction the train was headed. Only the names of the subway stations at either end of the line.

"Are you lost, young lady?" A man with rotted teeth and wearing a threadbare coat stood next to her. "Maybe I can help."

"No, thank you."

He took a step closer.

"Where are you going today, miss?"

Aurora didn't answer. She tried to move away from him, but the crush of waiting passengers didn't allow her much space to maneuver. If anyone noticed the man was bothering her, they weren't going to help.

"What stop are you looking for?" He kept after her.

Aurora squirmed past the people around her. She darted through an opening and found herself at the head of the line for an oncoming train. With its headlights shining through the darkness and horn blowing, Aurora only hoped it would get there before the man could catch up to her.

Screeching to a halt, the doors opened and the crowd stood back to let the riders off the train, except for Aurora, who dashed in to take a seat at the far end of the car.

"Please go, please go," she whispered, keeping her head lowered. Finally the whistle blew and the doors closed. Cautiously she took a look around. She didn't see the man until she heard a pounding on the window to her right. His face was pressed up against the glass, grinning wildly.

"Get used to it, sister." A woman sat down next to her as the train pulled out of the station. "Those derelicts live to see that reaction from you."

The woman wasn't much older than Aurora, and she was dressed in white from head to toe. She was carrying an American flag and a bouquet of roses.

"Until women get the right to vote," she said. "We'll never have a government that takes us seriously enough to clean up our cities and make it safe for us to ride the subway."

Aurora wasn't really listening. She was too worried about not having any idea as to where she was going.

"Excuse me, miss," she said. "Could you tell me if this is the train to Greenwich Village?"

"Why, of course it is." The lady seemed surprised by the question. "Take the Washington Square stop. I'm getting off there, too."

"Thank you." Aurora slumped down in her seat. At least she was going in the right direction.

"We're having a suffrage rally in the park today as people are getting off of work," said the woman. "You should join us."

Aurora leaned her head against the window and watched the tunnel walls whir by. Another time she might have considered the invitation. For now, she had to keep her mind on the purpose of this godforsaken trip. Finding Feldman's Fine Leather and then getting safely back to Fifty-Seventh Street.

As she emerged from the subway—the city's modern achievement or monstrosity, depending on your point of view—Aurora was immediately struck by the sensation that she had not only traveled in distance but also back in time.

The narrow streets of Greenwich were paved in cobblestone and lit with gas lamps. Ahead of her, a large marble arch rose above the entrance to Washington Square Park. Beyond it, she could see a dozen or so women in white waving their flags and chanting. Best to stay away from them, or she might get recruited by the lady from the train.

The pretzel stand on the curb was doing a brisk business with the office workers on their way home for the day, while children from the neighborhood were enjoying the temporary ice rink created around the park's main fountain. Aurora imagined herself gliding along, laughing with the other boys and girls as they tried out their skating moves. Too bad she didn't have time for such amusements. She glanced at her watch. Feldman's would be closing in just twenty minutes.

She reached into her pocket for the notes she'd made from Theo's directions. Feldman's Fine Leather, Ninety Reason Street. Or did he say Raisin? Whichever it was, if she walked west from the subway station he said she'd run right into it. But which way was west? Aurora made her best estimate by finding the afternoon sun and setting off in that direction.

She soon realized Greenwich didn't follow the usual grid pattern of New York City streets. The winding lanes were more suited for pushcarts than horse-drawn wagons, and not at all for automobiles. After awhile, the redbrick row houses behind their wrought iron fences all started to look the same, and Aurora had the feeling she was going around in circles. When she saw the Washington Square arch again, she knew she needed to ask for directions.

Someone at the pretzel stand should be able to help her. Aurora headed that way, until she got a closer look at one of the customers in line. It was her father, in his gray scarf and overcoat.

Seeing Father wasn't as much of a surprise as seeing who he was with. A woman with rosy red cheeks and short bob haircut was standing next to him. Father was whispering in her ear, and she was laughing. Then Father laughed. Her own father, who barely said two words around the house, was out with a strange woman and being charming to boot.

Aurora did an about-face before he could see her, hurrying away without knowing which way she was going. She could only think about why Father would be in Greenwich on a Monday afternoon. Wasn't his office nearer to City Hall? Or maybe his company had moved and he never mentioned it. But that still wouldn't explain the woman with him.

Eventually Aurora noticed that she had wandered onto a block full of small boutiques. Putting thoughts of her father aside, she wondered if she could be anywhere near Feldman's. She decided to walk to the next corner to look for a street marker, but she didn't have to go that far. The sign outside the shop just a few steps ahead read "Feldman's Fine Leather," and the woman inside was locking up for the day.

Aurora ran to the shop door and began knocking.

"Please, ma'am." She pointed to her watch. "It's not quite four. I'll only take a few minutes. Please."

The woman went on with her preparations for closing. She moved the expensive leather gloves out of the store's front window and drew together the shades.

Aurora kept knocking, now more forcefully. Theo had asked her to come all the way down here, and she wasn't about to be turned away by a clerk who wanted to leave early.

After a couple of minutes, the woman finally got annoyed enough to open the door. But only just a crack, to tell Aurora, "We're closed."

"But wait." Aurora pulled out the red leather glove from her bag. "It's important."

"Let me see that," said the woman, opening the door wider for a better look. "Where did you get it?" She reached out to rub the glove between her fingers. "This is made from one of our nicest leathers."

"I can explain," said Aurora. "If you'll just let me in."

The clerk reluctantly allowed her into the shop.

"What is it that you want, miss?" She was a tall woman wearing a high-collared black dress. Her graying hair was pulled back in a tight bun, making her thin face look even more severe.

Aurora drew a deep breath, taking in the leather fragrance of the shop. If Theo's theory about the owner of the glove was correct, she was going to have to play her part convincingly.

"This glove belongs to my aunt," she said.

"Is that so?" The woman's eyes narrowed. "How did you come by having it?"

"My aunt lost the mate to it, and she asked me to stop by the store and order her another."

The clerk didn't say anything. Instead, she turned away from Aurora and walked behind the counter. She pulled out a thick ledger book and started flipping through the pages.

"I remember this style distinctly," she said. "We only received a half-roll of the Isola red leather, one of the best on the market. They promised us more, but the shipment got stuck in customs. After that, we had to use a side leather. Still nice, but not nearly as fine as the Isola."

The clerk might be a pain, but she did know her business.

"Let's see here." The woman traced the names listed in the book with her finger. "We only sold a few pairs from that lot, back in early November."

She looked up at Aurora.

"What did you say your aunt's name was?"

Darn. If she gave Miss Powell's name and it wasn't on the list, the clerk would know that she'd been making up the whole story.

"Miss, your aunt's name?"

"My aunt's name is Maud Powell," said Aurora. "You may have heard of her. She's the famous violinist."

"Powell. Maud Powell." The clerk read through the names on the register. "I have Simon, Keller, Randolph, two pairs for Lewis."

Lewis must have been her father, but her mother would never wear something so youthful as a pair of red gloves. Could he have bought the second pair for that woman in the park?

"Then Lowenstein and Turner," said the clerk. "I don't see a Powell here."

"Turner?" asked Aurora. That sounded familiar. Of course, the Philharmonic program said Miss Powell was managed by her husband, Godfrey Turner.

"That's her, Maud Turner," said Aurora. "She's married to my dear Uncle Godfrey Turner. I forgot, she uses her maiden name as her stage name."

"Here she is. Maud Turner. The gloves were picked up by a courier."

The clerk looked at her.

"You say she lost the other one of the pair?" she asked, but Aurora wasn't listening.

How could Theo have been so sure the glove belonged to Miss Powell? And why was it important?

"Miss?"

"Sorry." Aurora stuffed the glove back into her bag. "Yes, she lost the right one and would like to have it replaced."

The clerk closed the accounting book.

"Unfortunately, as I said, we can't get any more of that particular leather."

She came around the counter.

"But we have several other attractive styles in our latest collection."

She stepped in front of one of the display cases and pointed to a pair of elegant gray suede gloves. With a prospective sale in sight, her concerns about the closing time had disappeared.

"Perhaps your aunt would like something more mature-looking than the red."

But Aurora was already heading to the door. She'd found out what she'd come for and needed to get back uptown to meet Theo and the boys.

"Thank you, ma'am," she said. "I'll let Auntie know she can't get a match."

"Please tell Mrs. Turner we've got plenty more to choose from," said the clerk. "And you too, miss. Come in anytime you're in the neighborhood."

Chapter 14

THE LATE AFTERNOON CROWD at Rosenberg's Deli was starting to thin out by the time Theo and the guys slid into their favorite booth in the back corner. If you didn't mind the bad food and surly service from the wait staff, Rosenberg's was a favorite hangout for Drama Academy students on a tight budget.

The greasy spoon's longtime waitress, Delores, shuffled up to their table. It was nearly her quitting time, and with her faded lipstick and annoyed look, she made sure everyone knew it.

"Aren't you kind of late today, fellas?" she asked. "It's way past you schoolboys' lunchtime."

"We was real busy today," said Eddie. "But we didn't want you to think we forgot about you."

"The usual?" she asked, not even bothering to take out her order pad. "Three pieces of pie and three coffees?"

"Make it four." Theo pointed to an empty place at the table. "We're expecting someone to join us."

"Just my luck. End of my shift and the big spenders show up." Delores moved along to spread her cheer to the next table of unsuspecting diners.

"Where is Aurora, anyway?" asked Eddie. "I hope something didn't happen to her."

"She should be here any time now," said Theo. "I wanted to go with her, but we had that darn elocution class this afternoon."

"I think she can take care of herself," said Bill. "At least, I hope so."

A couple minutes later, the young men sighed with relief as the diner's front door swung open. Aurora spotted them and headed for the back booth. Dropping her book bag on the floor, she slid in next to Theo and laid her head down on the table.

"You wouldn't believe the day I've had."

To her captivated audience, Aurora told of her escapades through the streets and subways of New York, ending up at Feldman's leather shop and confirming the owner of the red glove.

"Then it is true," said Bill.

"For some reason, I hoped it wouldn't be," said Theo.

"Why, what's the matter?" asked Aurora. "Miss Powell lost her glove and you found it. Anyone can lose a glove."

"There's more to it than that," said Theo.

"Actually, Eddie found it," said Bill. "He's the one who thought it was yours."

"Not really, Aurora." Eddie looked embarrassed. "I wouldn't think that of you."

"Isn't anyone going to tell me what you're talking about?" she asked.

"Eddie found the glove in the professor's studio," said Theo.

Aurora looked him curiously. "You didn't tell me that."

"We went back there on Saturday afternoon." Bill piped in. "After we saw you at the Plaza Hotel."

"You mean you went without me?" asked Aurora. "You didn't tell me that either, Theo."

"You had to get home, remember?" he said.

"Eddie found the glove in a closet the professor used to sleep in." Bill went on with the story. "There was some money in it."

"A lot of money," said Eddie.

Aurora tried to follow what they were saying.

"The professor slept in his studio, and since the glove is Miss Powell's, she was in the professor's studio?" she asked.

Eddie nodded.

"She probably was the lovely lady we saw on Saturday morning," said Bill. "Before you came in."

"You think so? Well, maybe she was taking a lesson," said Aurora.

"Without her violin?" Theo asked quietly.

"Oh my." She finally got it. "Miss Powell and the professor? That's silly. He would have been too old for her."

"Stranger things have happened," said Bill. "Look at Caesar and Cleopatra."

"Didn't turn out so well for them," said Eddie.

"My point exactly," said Bill.

"How would Miss Powell and Professor Schmieder even know each other?" As soon as Aurora asked the question, she knew the answer. Miss Powell had studied in Europe, in the professor's hometown of Heidelberg.

"I heard a couple of musicians talking about an argument they had in her dressing room before the concert Friday night," said Theo.

"Argument about what?" asked Aurora.

Theo shrugged his shoulders. "Let's just say Maud Powell is a lady of interest."

"A lady of so many interests," said Bill.

Aurora started to ask what he meant but thought better of it. She wasn't so sure she wanted to find out everything about Miss Powell.

The group fell silent.

"I think we need to know more about the professor before we jump to any conclusions," Theo said finally. "We should visit the cabaret club where he played."

"All right," said Eddie, smiling broadly. "I can get us in tomorrow night."

"Hold on, you're not going without me," said Aurora. "Not when I'm the reason you're doing all this. But I can't go traipsing around the city at all hours."

The foursome got quiet again.

"Wait, don't they have shows in the afternoon?" Theo asked Eddie.

"Sure." Eddie's shoulders drooped. "But the matinees aren't nearly as good."

Theo turned to Aurora. "You could come then, couldn't you?"

She hesitated. After making a point about wanting to be included, what was she getting herself into?

"Ahem," said Bill. "We're overlooking an important detail. The patrons at these kinds of places are usually all men. Working-class stiffs who want to let off some steam. If Aurora waltzes in there with her fair skin and long red hair, she'll probably cause a riot."

Oh dear, she thought. *This is sounding worse and worse.*

Theo thumped his fist on the table. "What's the matter with us? We're acting students and what do we know best? Putting on makeup and playing somebody else. We'll dress Aurora like a guy, smudge up her face some, and make sure her hair is under a hat."

She looked at him incredulously. "Do you expect me to ride the subway down to the East Side looking like that?"

Theo shook his head. "Eddie said the club is near his family's apartment. We can meet there first and then you can get ready. It's a cinch."

"Oh no, you don't," said Eddie. "Not in our crummy walkup, what with the kids running all around and laundry piled up."

"You want to help out Aurora, don't you, Eddie?" asked Theo. "After all, she's the one on the hook for the professor." He sat back in the booth. "But if you don't care about what happens to her, I guess we'll have to think of something else."

Eddie grumbled for a minute before giving in. "All right, but we can't let my ma know where we're going. She has a thing against Finkelstein's, says it brings in the wrong kind of people to the neighborhood."

Great, thought Aurora. *Even his mother thinks it's a bad idea.*

"But my sister should be home in the afternoon," Eddie said to her. "She's about your age and can help you change. Plus, she knows all about makeup and that kinda stuff."

"Then it's settled," said Bill. "All for one and one for all. Something like that."

Aurora stayed quiet. She didn't want to think about how she was going to get this one past Mother.

The tired-looking waitress was making her way to their table with a fresh pot of coffee and four pieces of toffee cream pie.

"Anything else for you millionaires?" she asked, setting out the last plate. "Or can I go home now?"

The boys were already chin-deep in their slices, so Aurora sent her on her way.

"Aren't you going to have any?" asked Eddie, after he came up for air.

"I can't," said Aurora. "It's almost suppertime."

She didn't add that she was dreading the conversation her family would be having as they passed around the roast beef and mashed potatoes. Trying to describe the finishing school when she had really been blocks away, or seeing her father in Washington Park. *Have a nice day at work, Father? Take any walks with a certain someone?*

Then on top of everything, making up another excuse for tomorrow.

"Come on, live a little," said Bill. "You should eat dessert whenever you feel like it. Who's going to stop you?"

"Oh, what the heck." Aurora dove into the creamy filling. She had a feeling a ruined appetite would be the least of her problems at the dinner table tonight.

Chapter 15

NEARLY HALF PAST SIX. Mother and Father would be livid. There was no way Aurora could convince them that she had been at the finishing school until this late. If Mother picked up on any hint of deception, she'd be talking with Lucy Stevens's mother to get the real story.

Best to try to avoid her parents until dinner at seven. To that end, she headed for the back entrance of their apartment, which led to the hallway outside the bedrooms.

Before turning the doorknob, she said a silent prayer. No matter how often Father reminded their housekeeper to lock the door, she usually forgot when she brought in the cleaning supplies or ran errands for Mother.

Please let this be one of those times.

With a gentle twist, the door eased open. Good old Nellie. Sweet, forgetful Nellie.

But what about her muddy boots? She couldn't mar the shiny floors with a track of footsteps leading straight to her bedroom door. As quiet as a mouse, she slipped off her boots and carried them. Odd that the hall light was on, even though it looked like there wasn't anyone in this part of the apartment. Another bit of luck.

In two shakes Aurora was down the hall and into her bedroom. She tossed her book bag on the dresser then searched for a place to stash her boots until she could clean them. Under the bed seemed the only choice. She dropped down to her hands and knees and pushed the boots as far under as possible.

She could say she'd come home from the finishing school and went straight to her room to do her lessons. Hopefully Mother had been in the kitchen preparing supper since getting back from the salon, not even noticing she was missing. Aurora had never told as many fibs in her whole life, much less all in one day. And she still had to come up with a whole set of new ones for tomorrow.

She didn't notice the tiny lady standing in her bedroom doorway until she got up from the floor.

"My gosh, Grandmother. You scared the daylights out of me."

Her grandmother, usually full of smiles and endearments, wasn't smiling now.

"Aurora, I've been worried about you."

She stepped into the room and closed the door.

"You wouldn't believe how time just flew by." Aurora tried to make light of the situation. "I sat in on a needlepoint class and didn't realize it was getting so late."

Grandmother shook her head, as if to say "don't even try." Aurora might be able to fool her parents, but the old woman had seen too much of the world to fall for her tricks.

"Your mother and father were asking for you," she said.

"They were?" asked Aurora.

"I told them you were resting in your room, and you asked not to be disturbed before supper. That's why I unlocked the back door for you, hoping you would be smart enough to avoid an embarrassing situation."

Aurora hung her head in shame. She had Grandmother lying for her as well.

"Don't be late for dinner." The elderly woman turned to leave. "By the way," she said. "Your mother is so pleased with your change of heart about the finishing school, she's starting to see the merits of you playing a musical instrument, as part of your education in becoming a proper young lady."

Aurora couldn't believe what she was hearing.

"Miss Powell is speaking at the museum luncheon your mother is going to later this week," Grandmother went on. "I may have suggested to her that it would be a nice feather in her cap if she could introduce herself to Miss Powell and let her know how delighted she is to have her daughter performing in her master class."

"Mother is going to meet Maud Powell?" Aurora hurried over to hug her grandmother. "You're absolutely marvelous."

"But you'll have to keep up your part of the bargain," said Grandmother. "At dinner tonight, do your best to look enthusiastic. Say a few nice things about your visit to the finishing school." She winked. "With your imagination, I'm sure you'll be able to come up with something."

A half hour later, with her story about the needlepoint class now well rehearsed, Aurora headed toward the dining room. But just before she entered, loud voices caused her to wait. Mother and Father were having one of their dinnertime "discussions." Only this was different, there was a third voice in the heated conversation.

"Son, I don't think I need to tell you, you're making a terrible mistake."

Aurora had never heard her grandmother join in an argument before, but tonight she was right in the middle of one.

"Mother, you don't understand how I feel." Aurora's father sounded more defeated than defiant. "First I had to grow up trying to live up to your standards, and I made a dismal failure of that. Then I married a woman who's doing the same thing to me."

Aurora thought she heard a sob. Mother? That stoic face of propriety was giving in to tears?

"You're a grown man, Winston, with a family to support," said Grandmother. "It's too late for you to be talking about feelings, as if you were a lovesick boy."

"But that's how I feel when I'm around Angeline."

Angeline? Was she the woman in the park?

"I will not have my house disgraced by such talk." Grandmother cut him off. "And don't forget, this is still my house."

"How could I, when you remind me of it every single day?"

What was Aurora to do? She couldn't walk right in; then they would know she had heard everything. Instead, she silently retraced her steps back to her bedroom. She quietly opened her door and then shut it with a bang as if she was just leaving her room. Coming down the hallway again, she used the foot-stomping walk that always irritated Mother.

To be even more noticeable, she whistled the melody from the "Romanze" in such a piercing tone she was sure they could hear it in the next apartment.

When she got to the dining room for the second time, Mother was setting the roast out on the table. She was sniffling and the rims of her eyes were red. On impulse, Aurora dropped a kiss on her cheek in greeting. Something she hadn't done since she was a girl of ten.

"Goodness, child," said Mother, nearly dropping the platter to the floor.

Father was seated at the head of the table. Aurora sat down in her place across from Grandmother, who was busy polishing her silverware with her napkin.

Mother set out the bowl of mashed potatoes and took her chair opposite Father.

"Winston?" she asked. "Could you lead us in a prayer of thanks for this lovely food and lovely home?" Her voice was as hard as nails. Any lapse into vulnerability had only been temporary.

Aurora stole a glance at her father as he mumbled a few words. She remembered how he looked in Washington Square, smiling and laughing. At home he was a downtrodden man hiding behind his glasses and evening paper, trying to keep out of the way of the women in his life. Aurora couldn't think of the last time she had seen him really happy, until this afternoon.

No matter what he had done, her heart ached for him. If that's what it meant to be a grown-up, Aurora wasn't so sure she was in a hurry to get there.

Chapter 16

"Busy again after school today, Aurora?" Lucy Stevens asked as they walked to the lunchroom.

"I'm visiting a friend of mine. She doesn't live in this neighborhood," added Aurora, just in case Lucy got nosy.

But "hmm" was all that Lucy said.

"My mother mentioned the finishing school that you go to," said Aurora, trying to be friendly as well as pick up a few details about the place in case her parents asked. Although in the chilly atmosphere at home, she doubted they would notice her coming in late for a second day in a row.

"How do you like the classes there?"

"You mean at Miss Evelyn's?" said Lucy. "They're okay, I guess."

Aurora was surprised by the lukewarm answer. She expected Lucy to be a more enthusiastic student.

"How often do you go there?"

"Mondays and Thursdays, and the tea parties on Saturdays. Mother just loves those tea parties." Lucy paused. "Would you like to come with me on Thursday?"

Uh-oh, thought Aurora. *Spend the afternoon making polite conversation with girls like Lucy Stevens?*

"I don't know," she said. "I mean, we're in school all day, and then I have to practice my violin."

"Aurora, you're so funny," said Lucy. "We don't have school on Thursday or Friday this week. It's a teacher's holiday, don't you remember?"

"Really?" asked Aurora. She had been so caught up in the commotion surrounding Professor Schmieder she'd forgotten all about the short school week.

"Of course," said Lucy. "Haven't you noticed Miss Ferrier has been in a good mood all morning?"

So that's why their teacher looked like she'd let out her corset a notch.

"On Thursday, I'm going to the women's club luncheon with Mother at the museum," said Lucy. "Then I'll walk over to Miss Evelyn's for the table-setting class. Who would have thought it was so complicated to serve dinner?"

With Lucy chattering away, a brilliant idea came to Aurora. Wasn't Mother going to the luncheon at the museum, too? Where Maud Powell was going to be the guest speaker?

It was a perfect plan. She would attend the luncheon with Mother and find a way to talk with Miss Powell alone. She doubted the violin soloist would remember her from their brief meeting backstage at Carnegie Hall. But Aurora had a feeling she would recognize the red glove from Feldman's Fine Leather.

Seeing Miss Powell's reaction would be worth suffering through all of Mother's fussing over what she should wear. And to top it off, she would be making her mother happy.

Maybe there was some advantage to thinking of others before yourself.

Chapter 17

"EMMA, ARE YOU IN there?"

Aurora stayed a step behind Eddie as he drew aside the hanging bedsheet, revealing a little cubbyhole off the tiny kitchen in his family's apartment. Behind her, Eddie's heavyset mother was busy keeping the pots on the wood-burning stove from boiling over, wiping perspiration from her forehead while a toddler pulled at her apron strings for attention.

"Em," Eddie said a little louder.

Looking over his shoulder, Aurora could see into the cramped alcove. Like all teenage girls, Eddie's sister must have needed some privacy. Only for Emma, that was behind bags of potatoes and onions in the family's food pantry. An unframed mirror hung above a vanity made of apple crates, and a clothesline strung across the narrow space held the girl's few nicely pressed but obviously hand-me-down dresses.

Aurora silently promised never to complain again about her bedroom at home, or having to wear any of the clothes Mother picked out for her.

"Em, are you awake?" asked Eddie.

On a low-slung cot, Aurora could see a girl with long dark hair lying face down, her head buried in a lumpy pillow.

"Go away," she said, not moving.

"What's the matter?" Eddie stepped in closer, but Aurora stayed where she was.

"What do you care if I end up an old maid?" the motionless girl muttered.

"Is that no-good Herbert bothering you again?" he asked. "Do you want me to punch his lights out once and for all?"

"That would be just perfect," said Emma. "When it gets around the neighborhood that my brother is a bully, I'll never have another boyfriend." She pounded the cot with her fists. "I'll end up working at the factory like Cousin Esther."

Eddie looked back at Aurora and rolled his eyes. She got the feeling he'd been through this routine before.

"Emma, I've got somebody here I want you to meet."

The flying fists suddenly stopped.

"Here, right now?" she asked quietly.

"My friends from the drama school came over. With the girl I told you about, Aurora Lewis."

Emma slowly sat up. Smoothing her hair down into place, Aurora could see the resemblance to Eddie in her broad face and dark eyebrows. But Emma was the first girl their age she had ever seen wearing real mascara, only now it was smeared in dark circles under her eyes.

Trying to act casual, Emma stood up and extended her hand.

"Sorry for my little tantrum. Nice to meet you, Aurora."

"Nice to meet you, too."

"Remember what I told you about, Em?" asked Eddie. "We need to turn Aurora into a fella for a couple of hours. Can you do it?"

Emma gave Aurora a long look. "You sure you want to go through with this?" she asked. "Finkelstein's can be kinda rough, even during the early shows."

"I'm sure," said Aurora, trying to sound confident. After what she'd been through in the past few days, she figured she could face anything.

"Remember, Em, I told Ma we're doing this for a school play," said Eddie. "You can't say anything to her about where we're really going. You know our deal, right?"

Emma looked toward Aurora with a big smile. "He promised me a fancy hat from the front window of Bloomingdale's for my birthday. With peacock feathers and everything."

"No need to gloat about it," said Eddie. "That plucked bird is going to cost me a good chunk of my baseball card collection. But can you turn Aurora into a guy?"

Emma took a step back to consider the task.

"It won't be easy," she said. "You're lucky Finkelstein's is pretty dark, even during the afternoon."

"I figured she could wear my brown suit, if she buckles up the belt real tight," said Eddie. "And I've got some boots she can slip over her regular shoes."

Aurora felt like a paper doll they were using to try on different outfits.

"What should we do with her hair?" asked Emma.

"That's a tough one," said Eddie. "I think I've got a black bowler big enough to tuck it all in."

"Such beautiful hair," said Emma, lightly touching the red waves. "Shame to pin it up."

Aurora felt the same way, but she would suffer if she had to.

"Can you do something about her face?" asked Eddie. "We need to scruff her up so she blends in with the crowd."

Aurora prepared herself for the worst.

"I'll try," said Emma. She bent down to pull a pink box tied with a white ribbon out from under her bed. "I work at the Gimbels cosmetic counter on the weekends."

Aurora's eyes opened wide. "You mean you have a real job?"

"To help make some money for the family." Emma took the lid off the box to show her a neatly arranged collection of face powders, eyes shadows, and skin creams. "They give me some of the samples to take home if I like."

Aurora's eyes opened wider.

"Okay, I can see you girls are in heaven," said Eddie. "I'll bring the clothes and let's see if you can turn Aurora into an Arthur."

"Not bad, not bad," said Theo, stepping around her for a full circle view.

"As long as she keeps those dainty little hands in her pockets," said Bill.

"I think that hat looks better on her than me," said Eddie, pulling it down over Aurora's eyes.

From the corner of the kitchen, Eddie's mother glanced over at them but didn't say a word.

Emma took the mirror off her wall and handed it to Aurora, so she could see the results of the makeover.

Aurora gasped when she saw her reflection. With her darkened eyebrows, ashen cheeks, and penciled-in upper-lip hair, she looked like any other nondescript young clerk going to work. Emma had even used Aurora's school clothes for padding to help fill out her shape, although no one would mistake her for a bodybuilder.

"Wait, you're missing one thing," said Eddie, leaving the group for a moment.

"Remember," said Theo. "Talk in a low voice, or better yet, don't talk at all. Just stay behind me."

"Here you go." Eddie returned holding a pair of horn-rimmed glasses. "They're fake ones I picked up in case I ever need them for an acting part."

Aurora slipped the glasses on and Eddie nodded in approval.

"Now you look like a real *mensch*."

Chapter 18

"WELL, IT'S NO ZIEGFELD Follies," said Bill, pointing to the Finkelstein's club entrance at the top of the staircase. "Eddie, you conveniently forgot to tell us it's five flights up."

"Ah, quit being a smart aleck," said Eddie. "Hey, that's my buddy up there at the door. Yo, Abe!"

He zigzagged through the line of men waiting on the stairs, waving for Theo, Bill, and Aurora/Arthur to follow.

"I hope they don't get too mad at us for cutting ahead like this," said Bill as they elbowed their way through the crowd.

"I hope nobody yells 'Fire!'" Theo whispered to Aurora.

She held on to Theo's arm as they navigated up the stairs. She could barely see because Eddie's hat was pulled down so far over her eyes, and his loose-fitting overboots nearly slipped off every time she took a step. Dressed in his heavy coat and wool pants in the overly warm stairwell, she hoped she'd make it to the top without fainting.

"Hi ya." Eddie was all smiles when they finally made it to the front of the line. "Guys, this is my pal I told you about, Abe Finkelstein. He runs this fine establishment."

About as wide as he was tall, it was obvious why Abe was working double duty as the ticket seller and doorman. With wads of bills stuffed between his fat fingers, and a pockmarked face showing more than a few reminders of bygone fistfights, Abe wasn't someone you'd want to irritate. Theo and Bill let Eddie do all the talking. Aurora kept quiet, too, per her instructions.

"Abe, you ready to fix us up with your best table tonight?" Eddie puffed out his chest. "Me and my friends are looking for a good time."

Abe looked them up and down. "You fancy boys here to see the show? Even the scrawny one?" He pointed at Aurora. "He doesn't look old enough to be out of school yet."

Aurora nudged herself behind Theo and kept her eyes averted to the floor.

"Oh, you mean Arthur?" asked Eddie, without a hint of worry in his voice. "He's small for his age, but twice as ornery. We just came over from the academy."

"You still wasting time in that acting school, Manny?" asked Abe, forgetting about little Arthur. "Even going to the trouble of changing your name and for what? You could come work for me like I done asked you a long time ago. Ain't this show business enough for you?"

"It's a tempting offer, Abe, and don't think I don't appreciate it," said Eddie. "But I'm going to be in the talking pictures someday. That's why I've got to finish my studying."

"Now you're practicing to be a comedian." Abe laughed. "They're a dime a dozen around here."

"You'll see," said Eddie. "I'm going to be a big star. Then you'll be paying money to see me."

"But for now, you want to see my show for free?"

For a moment, Abe looked seriously annoyed but then broke out into another hearty roar.

Eddie laughed along with him. Bill, Theo, and Aurora smiled to be polite, even though the crowd behind them was starting to get agitated.

"Lucky you came for the early show," said Abe. "Otherwise, I'd have to charge you. But we're trying out a couple of new acts, so I'll let you in on the house. Afterward, I want to get your educated opinion on our performers."

"Not a problem," said Eddie.

"All right, pretty boys. The first number's about to go on." Abe moved aside to let them through the door. "My hostess, Lula, will get you a table. And remember to drink plenty. That's not included in the free admission."

"No worries there," said Eddie. "Come on, fellas, let's get inside."

It took a few seconds for Aurora's eyes to adjust to the darkness of the theater, if you could rightfully call it that. As best as she could make out, they were in a former warehouse with a makeshift bar set up in the back. The seating consisted of wooden chairs behind long picnic tables. The stage in the front of the room was set on a platform three or four feet above the audience.

The floor was sticky, the result of too many beer tosses and too few mops. The foul odor of stale brew mixed with mildew was enough to prompt Bill to take out his handkerchief and cover his nose.

"Are you crazy?" Eddie swiped down Bill's hand. "They're about to toss us out as it is, without you asking for it."

Bill's usual sarcastic response was cut short by the appearance of the theater's hostess. Although her face was a few years too old for the dance revue, she was still packing all the essentials in her silver-beaded gown, cut low in the front and high on the leg.

"I'm Lula. Are you friends of Abe's?"

When she smiled, she displayed a gap where her front tooth should have been. "Floor show's gonna start in a few minutes. Follow me, boys."

Focusing on Lula as she weaved through the club, they arrived at one of the few private tables in front of the stage.

"Here you are, gentlemen. Best view in the house." Lula gestured for them to take their seats. "Miriam will be here to get your order. She'll take good care of you."

They barely had time to settle into their chairs when a waitress popped up beside them. With straight black hair and a crooked nose, she looked like one of those young women who'd been given little choice in life except to grow up too soon. She wore thick makeup and tight-fitting clothes, but she had one distinguishing feature that would keep her from ever working on the stage: a set of buckteeth that would have impressed even a jackrabbit.

"My name's Miriam." She mumbled through a wad of gum stuffed into her cheek. "What'll you have?"

"I'll have an old-fashioned." Bill jumped in. "With a slice of orange."

The waitress stared at him blankly, chewing away on her Wrigley's.

"Bring us a pitcher of beer." Eddie settled the matter. "Here." He slipped a dime into the girl's hand. "Be quick about it."

Without another word, Miriam plodded away.

She's not any older than me, thought Aurora. *While I'm sipping sodas after school with my girlfriends, Miriam is working for tips at Abe's.*

"Look." Theo pointed to the back of the stage, where the musicians were setting up for their first number. The trio included a piano, drums, and violin. "They found a replacement for the professor pretty quick."

To get the crowd's attention, the band launched into a ditty from a Scott Joplin rag. Or at least the piano player and drummer did. The violinist, in a rumpled jacket and his hair uncombed, looked like he'd just rolled out of bed. And his playing wasn't much better than his appearance.

"He's terrible," said Aurora, keeping her voice low. "They must have been desperate to get someone to fill in." Though she still couldn't believe her teacher had played in a place like this.

Even an uncultured audience can tell the difference between a melody and cat scratching. By the end of the second stanza, the men around them were hissing and booing.

"Tough crowd," said Theo, gesturing for Aurora to keep her head down in case the customers started throwing their empties.

Thankfully the emcee for the show took center stage and cut off the music. A short, stout man who looked like a smaller version of Abe, he motioned for the crowd to quiet down.

"Good afternoon, everyone." He strained to be heard above the racket. "Thanks for showing up."

"That's Abe's cousin," said Eddie. "Benny Finkelstein."

"We've got a fine show for you. Comedy."

The booing got louder.

"Singing."

So did the hissing.

"And of course, our lovely chorus line of dancing girls."

Cheers went up all around.

"Now let's give a nice round of applause for a new act here at the club, Lahr and Mercedes."

Tepid clapping welcomed a bumbling policeman stumbling onto the stage. He was wearing high-water pants and an oversized jacket, and carrying a Billy club in one hand while with the other he adjusted a pint-sized hat on his bowling ball–sized head. But the crowd responded much more favorably when a pretty lady dressed in a dancer's tutu appeared before them.

"Just a minute there, miss." The policeman slurred through his words. "We don't allow no racy dancin' in this town."

"Boo!" The crowd roared.

"Let her dance," someone called out, to everyone's approval.

On cue, the woman gave her hips a wide swing, accompanied by a drumroll and cymbal crash.

"But, Officer." Her whiny voice cut through the din of the nightclub. "I just gotta dance." She shimmied under his nose. "I just gotta."

The policeman turned to the audience.

"Some fun, eh, folks? Nyuk, nyuk, nyuk."

For another ten minutes the soused cop and addleheaded hoofer entertained the crowd. Whenever there was a lull in the performance, the comic would go into a series of one-liners and face contortions that brought down the house.

"Do you know who that guy is?" Theo asked Eddie.

"Irving Lahrheim," said Eddie. "He grew up a couple streets over from me. He's about our age."

"Is that so?" Theo took a closer look. "He's not half-bad."

"He started out in some kid's show about a year ago," said Eddie. "Since then he's been working with this Mercedes gal."

After a short round of exit music from the band, the houselights went up for a break between the acts. A skinny kid with big ears was pushing a Statue of Liberty cutout onto the stage for the set change. Miriam came back with their drinks, while other customers were lining up for a refill at the bar.

"I'm going to talk to the piano player," said Theo. "You want to come?" he asked Aurora.

She nodded and stood up. At least her disguise stayed in place.

"I'm going backstage to say 'hello' to Benny," said Eddie. "I'll let him know how much we like the show."

Bill didn't offer an opinion. He was resigned to sitting back in his chair with a tortured look on his face.

The piano player didn't have much to say about the professor, and even less good to say about him.

"Schmieder was a pain, no two ways about it. Always with the 'I'm better than you' attitude. But he showed up every night, I'll give him that. He was a lot better than the *schlemiel* we have playing the strings tonight."

"Did you notice anything unusual about the professor?" asked Theo. "Any strange characters ever come around to see him?"

The piano man laughed.

"Look around you, sonny. Everyone here is a strange character. Nah, Schmieder kept to himself. Played his music, picked up his pay, and left."

He plinked on the keyboard.

"We've got to get started again," he said. "Benny doesn't like it if the crowd gets too restless."

"Just one more thing," said Theo. "How did you find out the professor died?"

"Abe sent a messenger over to my place around noon on Saturday. Kid woke me up, too. Told me I needed to find a new fiddler for the night show."

"But how did Abe find out?" asked Theo.

The piano player shrugged. "Abe always has a line on what's going on in the city."

With the crowd starting to take their seats, Theo and Aurora headed back to their table.

"I wonder how Abe could have found out so quickly about Professor Schmieder," said Theo. "Even the manager at the Palm Court didn't know until I told him in the afternoon."

"I can't help you with that," said Aurora. "But did you notice the kid on the stage, the one who was pushing out the Statue of Liberty?"

"I wasn't paying attention to him," said Theo.

"He reminded me of somebody," said Aurora.

"There you are." Eddie called out to them. "Look who we have here."

Two young women had joined their group. "Let me introduce you to our new friends," said Eddie. "This is Candy. She's dancing in the chorus line later in the show."

A blonde with a painted face giggled. "Aren't you cute?" she asked, chucking Eddie under the chin.

"And that's Suzette." Eddie pointed toward to the femme fatale sitting close to Bill. Somewhere in that long, ravishing dark hair, Aurora was sure Bill had forgotten how much he hated this place.

The house lights dimmed and Benny the emcee was onstage again. Theo and Aurora took their seats, trying their best to avoid looking at the canoodling couples sitting next to them.

"Welcome back, gentlemen." He paused. "And ladies." Benny nodded to the front table. "Looks like everyone is starting to have a good time."

A rim shot startled Bill loose from Suzette's embrace. With his hair standing every which way and red lipstick dotting his face, soon the whole front of the theater was laughing at his dazed appearance.

Everyone was in on the joke except Eddie. He was in a deep philosophical discussion with his blonde minx. Punctuated with nibbles on her nose.

"That's why we're here folks, to have a good time." Benny nodded approvingly. "All right, next we've got a very special treat for you. A little lady who's going to be a big name in show business someday. Let's give a warm welcome to our very own Miss Fanny Brice!"

"Oh, no!" said Eddie, disengaging from Candy's clutches. "I know her."

He slid his chair behind Theo's.

"That's Fania Borach." Eddie sounded like he was hyperventilating. "Her ma and mine are best friends in the neighborhood. If she sees me here, I'm dead."

Lucky for Eddie, the lights in the club were all turned on the—well, "beautiful lady" wasn't quite the right description for the woman taking the stage. Standing in front of the Lady Liberty cutout, Fanny was dressed in a striped black-and-white dress decorated with a plume of white feathers of indeterminate origin. She stood with her chin perched on her forefinger and her mouth turned downward in a frown. With her wide brown eyes and prominent nose, she wasn't a classic beauty, but she certainly held everyone's attention.

The crowd quieted, in anticipation of what would happen next.

A sly smile emerged on the entertainer's lips.

"I was just saying to myself the other day, 'Fanny, when are you going to settle down and get married? What's taking so long?'" She winked at the audience.

"I got a nice figure, don't I?"

The crowd gave a mixed review.

"My legs ain't half-bad." She lifted up her skirt to show her knock-knees. The crowd laughed along with her.

"My face." She turned sideways to give them a full view of the nose of Gibraltar. "That could use some work, I do admit. But one thing you've got to give me credit for, I can sing."

She turned to the band.

"Hit it, boys."

A couple minutes into Fanny's opening number, Eddie leaned forward and whispered to Theo and Aurora. "I've got to get out of here."

"What?" Theo looked back over his shoulder. "You're not leaving us with lover boy over there."

He nodded toward Bill, who was slumped over in his chair, feeling the effects of the lady and the liquor.

On stage, the music stopped.

"My mother always told me, 'Fanny, forget about all that show business stuff. Find a nice boy.'"

Then she paused, looking intently beyond the stage. Theo tried to sit up taller to hide his friend, but it was too late.

"Oh, no." Eddie groaned.

"Is that you, Emanuel?" Fanny shielded her eyes from the stage lights so she could get a better look.

Eddie covered his face with his hands.

"What are you doing in here?" Fanny's voice buzzed through the crowd noise like one of those drilling machines at the construction site on Forty-Second Street.

"Wait until your mama hears about this."

Detective O'Shea sat a few tables back from the stage, taking in the banter between Fanny and the embarrassed audience member. He knew Theo Eckstein and his sidekicks but didn't recognize the other young man with them. Not until he saw a wisp of red hair slipping out from under her black hat.

He knew it wasn't a coincidence that Aurora Lewis had dressed up like a boy to make a visit to Finkelstein's. They were all on the same track, checking out where the professor used to make his extra pocket money.

Even though the spectacle at the front table was good entertainment, the real story was taking place backstage. That's where the stagehand with the big ears had disappeared to. O'Shea knew him right off the bat. He was the young fellow who'd accused Aurora Lewis of pushing Professor Schmieder out the window.

But why had a Bowery Boy been all the way uptown when the professor took his tumble into the alley?

Chapter 19

Detective O'Shea wandered into the police station around three in the afternoon. Wednesday was his day off, but after sleeping in until noon and then having lunch at the automat a couple doors down from the boarding house, there wasn't much else to do to fill up the time until dinner.

Unlike the shiny new stations the department was opening on the city's north side, the midtown precinct still had old cinder-block walls and wooden benches in the waiting area. Watched over by a lone sergeant sitting at the front desk, counting the hours until his shift was over.

"What do you know, Joe?" asked O'Shea.

"Nothing." Sergeant Donovan didn't look up from reading the latest issue of the *NYPD Review*. Behind which, O'Shea figured, was the race card for the horses running today out at Belmont Park.

"Doesn't look too busy in here." The detective pointed at the empty benches.

"No lines, no waiting."

Donovan didn't answer. Most desk men usually didn't show much interest in anything other than depositing their paycheck with the nearest bookie.

"How about last night, any interesting calls?" asked O'Shea, scanning the police blotter. "What's this?" He pointed to an entry. "Someone reported a burglary in one of the offices at the Knickerbocker Theater. Says here they were trying to steal a violin?"

Donovan sighed in exasperation and laid down his magazine, letting the tearsheet for a two-year-old filly slip out from under the cover.

"Yeah, heard about it when I came in today," he said. "Turns out the guy is a manager for some music acts. He left the violin in his office when he and his wife went to dinner. She's a musician with the orchestra. Anyway, when they got back from the restaurant, the transom over the door was broken and the place was ransacked."

"Did the burglars get the violin?" asked O'Shea.

"No, just a couple cameras and some small jewelry," said Donovan. "They found the violin lying on the floor, dumped out of its case. Captain thinks the burglars were scared off because they didn't expect anyone to come back that night. They hightailed it out of there using the fire escape but left the fiddle."

O'Shea took another look at the entry. "The guy's name is Turner. Godfrey Turner. I know that name from somewhere."

"Captain thinks this job might be related to the robbery that happened at the opera house a few weeks ago," said Donovan. "Only over there they got away with the violin."

"Probably a nice little payoff, too," said O'Shea. "If you know the right buyer, could be worth a couple thousand."

"Dollars? For a violin? That's crazy," said Donovan.

Then he went back to his reading.

O'Shea stood there thinking for a minute.

"Did you see Sergeant Daley come in today?" he asked.

"Sure, he just walked through," said Donovan. "He's got the afternoon shift for patrol."

"Get him for me," said O'Shea, pointing to the black phone on the desk.

Donovan put down his magazine again and dialed the number. He handed over the receiver when the call was picked up.

"Daley, this is O'Shea. Is that report on the Schmieder case still on my desk?"

He knew it would be because Daley was notorious for never doing the filing when he was supposed to.

"You mean the guy who fell out of the window at the Carnegie Towers?" asked Daley.

"That's the one," said O'Shea. "Does it say anything in the file about a violin being in the studio? Either lying out or in a case?"

O'Shea didn't have to wait for an answer.

"I don't need to look at the file," said Daley. "I saw the black violin case myself, sitting next to the door. What about it?"

O'Shea didn't respond.

"Detective?" asked Daley.

"I want you to go back over to the studio today before you start patrol," said O'Shea. "See if that violin is still in there."

"Ah, come on, Barney," said Daley. "You know the captain closed the case. We're not supposed to do anything more with it."

"I don't care, I gave you an order," said O'Shea. "And another thing, did you and the crew wreck that place when you were searching it on Saturday? I was over there later in the afternoon and it looked like a tornado had come through."

"No way," said Daley, his voice rising. "We left everything nice and neat. I made sure of it."

"All right, I believe you," said O'Shea. "Just go back there and check on the violin."

He hung up the phone and went back to his thinking mode.

If Daley didn't tear up the studio, then Theo and his buddies had some explaining to do. He'd bet a fiver that they'd been back to the professor's on Saturday before he saw them coming off the elevator in the Carnegie Hall lobby. But more important, something about that violin struck him as off-kilter. Because he couldn't remember seeing it when he went up to the professor's studio that same afternoon.

Chapter 20

AURORA HAD BEEN SITTING on the wooden bench outside the Drama Academy for more than an hour, and it was starting to get awfully hard. After getting home from school today, Grandmother told her that her piano accompanist, Mr. Eckstein, had called to remind her about their rehearsal that afternoon at the Carnegie Towers. Grandmother never asked why Aurora would need an accompanist on a piece arranged for solo violin, or where this Mr. Eckstein had suddenly come from.

She didn't even have to do any explaining to Mother. She was too busy preparing Father's favorite dishes for dinner to do more than wave good-bye as Aurora walked out the door. She hadn't been around the house enough lately to know what accounted for Mother's change of heart, but at least they'd have some conversation at the dinner table tonight. She never thought she would actually miss hearing Mother going on about the latest town gossip.

But as she scanned the empty hallway, Aurora wondered if she had misunderstood Theo's secret message. If he wanted to see her, then why have her sit here all alone? Students had been coming and going, but there hadn't been any sign of the boys. And now it was eerily quiet, with only the clanking of the elevator to break the silence. Up and back down again, but never stopping on the fourth floor.

She eyed the violin case lying next to her on the bench. This was silly. She could be at home actually practicing for the master class instead of sitting here doing nothing. She hadn't played since last Saturday, and this afternoon was the first time she'd even taken her violin out of the closet. If she didn't get some real rehearsing in soon, her debut would be a disappointment for herself, Miss Powell, and the listeners.

"That's funny," she said out loud, taking a closer look at the case. She didn't remember it ever looking so immaculate. Where was that knick from when she accidentally bumped it into the radiator in her bedroom? Or the scratch from brushing up against the brick exterior of Carnegie Hall during one of her mad dashes to get to her lesson on time?

She turned the case on one side and then the other, sliding her hand over the rich grains in the black leather. She'd never paid attention before to how smooth it felt.

Aurora unlatched the lid and lifted it open. The first thing she noticed was that the picture she kept inside her case was missing, the one from Father's *Saturday Evening Post* of the girl holding three kittens. Then she saw the deep-purple velvet cloth lying over the violin. Which would have been fine, except the cover for her violin was dark green. The only person she knew who had a purple one was ...

She shut the lid in a panic and looked around. Now she was glad the boys were late and she was by herself.

Aurora took another peek into the case, gingerly lifting up the purple shroud.

"Oh no," she said. She placed her hand under the instrument but didn't pick it up. She already knew she was holding Professor Schmieder's Gagliano violin.

"Oh no," she said again. "How could this have happened?"

She thought about the last time she'd played her own violin. It had been before her lesson last Saturday. She'd been practicing the "Romanze" at home, and then she packed up and walked over to the Carnegie Towers. She knew she had her violin with her when she was talking with the boys in the hallway, and even when she let herself into the professor's studio. But she never got the chance to play for Professor Schmieder.

She looked toward the professor's closed studio door. Could she have somehow picked up her teacher's violin instead of her own during the confusion of that morning? Did that mean her violin was still in his studio? Maybe she could see if it was unlocked and switch them back.

Before she could make a move, the doors of the academy swung open. Out walked Theo, Bill, and Eddie, coming straight toward her.

She gently let go of the violin and closed the case, making sure the latches were securely fastened.

"I'm sorry," said Theo when they reached her. "The Elizabethan drama teacher decided to schedule a makeup exam for this afternoon, and I couldn't get a hold of you in time to let you know."

Aurora smiled weakly. Usually she would have made a fuss about being inconvenienced, but not today. Today she couldn't even speak.

"I hope you don't mind me calling your house with that story about a rehearsal," said Theo. "But I—I mean, *we*—wanted to know if you got in okay last night."

She nodded. After the scene between Eddie and Fanny at the club, the foursome had slunk out of Finkelstein's with a whimper. Rather than bother Eddie's family again by changing back into her school clothes there, she took the chance of riding home on the subway with Theo. Between the two of them, they got her face to a presentable state and unpinned all her hair. Then in case she needed an explanation for her parents as to why she was wearing men's clothes, they concocted a story about her being given the lead male role in a play at the all-girl finishing school, so naturally she had to dress for the part.

As it turned out, she could have waltzed into the apartment without any worries. Mother and Grandmother stayed in their bedrooms all evening, and Father didn't come home until late. After putting on her pajamas, Aurora ended up eating cold chicken for dinner and then going to bed.

"I didn't have any problems when I got home," she said to the boys. "And here, Eddie." She took a linen bag out of her school satchel. "I brought your clothes back. I tried to fold them for you." She handed the bag to him.

"No worries," he said. "You were a good sport about letting us dress you up."

"Do you still have some time to spend with us?" Theo pointed to his watch. "We were thinking of going over to Rosenberg's."

"After one of those tests, I'm famished," said Bill.

"Me too," said Eddie, patting his stomach.

Aurora hadn't planned on getting home late again, but she needed to tell them about the violin mix-up.

"All right," she said. "But there's something you should know."

Before she could say more, the elevator started making noise again. It found its way up to the fourth floor, where it ground to a jerky halt.

Once the doors opened, Aurora recognized the man stepping out as the younger officer who had been in the music studio taking their names after Professor Schmieder's fall. The sergeant walked past them complaining loudly about having to listen to that "fatso" detective. He stopped in front of the professor's studio, pulled out a key from his pocket and let himself in, grumbling all the way.

Aurora gave Theo a worried look. According to the official version from Detective O'Shea, the professor's death was considered an accident. If that was so, why was he sending his underling over here again?

For a moment, she considered following the policeman into the studio and telling him about the professor's violin. But if O'Shea was still chasing the idea that she was somehow involved in Professor Schmieder's death, having his valuable violin in her possession would only make things look worse for her.

"I think we should leave before the policeman comes back out," Theo said quietly. "Otherwise, he might wonder why we're all hanging around and start asking us questions."

Bill and Eddie nodded in agreement, which was fine with Aurora. Gripping the violin case tightly, she followed them to the elevator.

"I'm going to try something," said Theo. "Just play along with me."

After they stepped inside, the operator, the same little man in his same wrinkled brown suit, cranked the controls forward. The elevator doors creaked closed and Aurora held on for the bumpy ride.

"Long day, isn't it?" Theo asked the man. "Being on your feet the whole time with hardly a break."

At first the operator didn't know he was the one being talked to.

"They should put a stool in here for you to sit on," said Theo.

The man looked back at him but didn't say a word.

"What time do you start in the morning, anyway?" asked Theo.

"Nine o'clock sharp." The operator finally spoke up. "Never been late a day in five years. I'm here every day except Sundays."

"I bet you see all kinds of people, don't you? What with us crazy acting students and musicians running around."

Why is Theo asking him all these questions? Aurora thought. *Let the man do his job in peace.*

"Like last Saturday," Theo continued. "Do you remember a lady coming in before ten in the morning? She was wearing a very fashionable hat and dress. Very elegant."

Now Aurora knew what Theo was doing.

"That was almost a week ago," said the man. "My memory ain't so good."

Theo tapped him on the shoulder and extended his hand.

"My name's Theo," he said. "How about yours?"

"My name?"

"We see each other almost every day and I don't even know your name," said Theo.

The elevator slowed down as they approached the lobby.

Theo offered his hand again. This time, the man accepted.

"Maurice," he said with a slight smile.

"How about last Saturday morning, Maurice?" asked Theo. "You remember the lady I'm talking about now, don't you?"

"Oh yes, I never seen her around here before. She was mighty fancy, all done up in purple and wearing a fur coat."

"That's the one," said Theo. He turned to Aurora and mouthed the words "Maud Powell."

"But isn't she too old for you?" Maurice winked. "Not like this little gal." He nodded toward Aurora. "Pretty to look at and polite as can be. Always says 'please' and 'thank you.'"

Maurice isn't as dull as he first appeared, she thought.

"Much nicer than the skinny girl I brought up here on Saturday morning, just after I came on duty," he said. "She's been here a few times and always been rude to me."

The elevator car went silent.

"You mean you brought another girl up to the fourth floor that morning?" Theo finally asked.

"Yeah, she orders me around, telling me to 'hurry up' and 'open the door.'"

"What does she look like?" asked Theo.

"Skinny, with long, straight black hair and a set of awful buckteeth."

The elevator lurched to a halt on the ground floor.

"When did the girl with the black hair leave?" asked Theo as the doors opened.

"She never took the elevator down," said Maurice. "Neither did the fancy lady. Only took one-way rides."

Chapter 21

Aurora watched as Theo and the boys demolished a heaping plate of french fries at Rosenberg's Deli. But she didn't have the appetite to join in and instead swished around the black coffee in her coffee cup. She'd been waiting for the right time to tell them that the professor's violin was sitting right next to her in the booth. But they were still going over the unexpected information from the elevator operator.

"How did you get him to talk like that?" asked Eddie. "He usually never says a word."

"I slipped him a dollar when I shook his hand," said Theo. "When all else fails, use cash."

Eddie nodded in approval.

"But you know, Maurice's description of the girl reminded me of somebody," said Theo. "Long black hair, skinny."

"With buckteeth," said Bill. "You know who she is? Our waitress at Finkelstein's. Mary or Minnie."

"Miriam," said Aurora. "I remember her. I kept thinking she was my age."

"The professor was being friendly with the help over at Abe's?" asked Eddie. "I wouldn't have believed it."

"Yeah, even the piano player said he was in and out of there with barely a word to anyone," said Theo.

"You know, I noticed someone else over there," said Aurora. "The kid who was moving the props around on the stage during intermission." She looked at Bill and Eddie. "Did either of you see him?"

They sheepishly shook their heads.

"That's when they were getting acquainted with Candy and Sugar." Theo grinned.

"Candy and Suzette," said Bill with a dreamy look in his eyes. "Lovely young ladies."

"Anyway," said Aurora. "That stagehand was one of the troublemakers from the alley on Saturday. He was the one who said I pushed Professor Schmieder out the window. I'm sure of it."

"Really?" asked Theo. "The guy who was in the studio talking to Detective O'Shea, the one with the big ears?"

Aurora nodded. "So Miriam visits the professor early in the morning, and then that fellow is out in the alley just a little while later."

The boys stopped eating.

"But why would Miriam and that alley rat spend time with Professor Schmieder?" asked Eddie. "I know the kids in my neighborhood, and they wouldn't make friends with an old man just to be nice. And we know the professor wasn't rich."

But he did have something of value, thought Aurora, lightly touching the violin case.

Theo shrugged. "Even so, I'm starting to think again that Maud Powell has more to do with all of this. We still don't even know why she visited the professor on Saturday morning."

"But how are we going to find out anything about her?" asked Eddie.

"I'm going to her lecture tomorrow, that's how," said Aurora.

The boys looked at her in surprise.

"You are?" asked Eddie.

"I'm going with my mother to the women's club luncheon at the museum," she said. "Miss Powell is the guest speaker, and afterward I'm going to try to talk to her about the red glove, and the professor."

"Good job, Aurora." Theo patted her on the back. "You're the only who can speak to her directly. We'll be counting on you to bring us back a good story."

Aurora smiled. At least she could do something right.

"When should we meet again?" asked Theo. "Aurora, you tell us."

"Well, I'm off from school on Friday," she said. "I could say I need to go to the library."

Theo looked at her admiringly. "Friday is good for us, right, fellas?"

Bill and Eddie nodded in approval.

"Then we'll meet on Friday morning at the library," said Theo. "In the Rose Main Reading Room."

Chapter 22

Turning the corner from Rosenberg's, Aurora struggled against the cold wind whipping down Seventh Avenue. It was already getting dark, and although Theo had offered to walk her home, she knew he had a late class at school. Besides, she could make the few blocks on her own. No one knew what she was carrying.

After the boys had been so impressed with her plan to meet Miss Powell, she didn't have the heart to tell them about the professor's violin. Maybe they would think she did have a reason to harm Professor Schmieder. Or in the least, that she was such a foolish girl she didn't even know she'd been carrying the wrong instrument all this time. No, she would have to figure out a way to switch the violins on her own, without anyone else being the wiser.

Trudging along, she realized that in her absentminded way, she'd forgotten to bundle up before leaving the warm restaurant. She nearly lost her balance juggling the violin from one bare hand to the other, while at the same time trying to keep her hat from flying off her head. At this rate, she'd be as frozen as an ice cube by the time she got home.

Up ahead, she saw a doorway that would offer temporary shelter. The lightbulb above the portal was burned out, so she had to fumble around in the shadows to fasten all the buttons on her coat. She set down the violin to tie her hat on tight and put on her red gloves. Now she was ready to rejoin the winter march home. For a moment, she studied the slow progression of pedestrians down the sidewalk. Cloaked in black overcoats, with wisps of white breath rising above their heads, they looked like a great big lumbering steam locomotive. All moving together, yet each one very much alone.

No more dillydallying, she scolded herself. She reached down for the violin case. Only her hand came up empty.

"What the heck?" she asked aloud.

She turned to look behind her. The violin was gone. Professor Schmieder's violin was gone. It had been there just a second ago.

In alarm, she scanned the huddled figures trudging down the sidewalk. No one was carrying anything as obvious as a violin case. Then she saw a man running across the street through the traffic, holding something very familiar above his head.

"Thief, thief!"

Aurora ran into the road after him. Headlights shined in her face and brakes squealed all around her as she chased the robber, not wanting to lose sight of him when he reached the other side.

"Stop him. He stole the violin."

One of the automobile drivers shouted out his window.

"Hey, girlie. You're going to get yourself killed."

"He took the violin," she cried. "Someone's got to stop him."

Watching from the other side of the street, Detective O'Shea could make out Aurora Lewis as the young woman blocking traffic. He was about to call to her when he noticed Sticky Fingers Jones, midtown's resident pickpocket, slip in among the crowd just ahead of him, not so discreetly carrying a violin case.

O'Shea quickened his step until he was right behind Jonesy, who had slowed down a bit, probably thinking he had lost the girl. The detective let him take a couple more steps of freedom before he grabbed him by his frayed collar. Pulling him out of the wave of people, O'Shea pressed the scrawny thief up against the wall of the savings-and-loan building. He used his wide frame to discourage any ideas Jonesy might have about trying to slip away.

"Out of jail this afternoon and you're already back at work?" asked O'Shea.

Sticky Fingers never had a clean-shaven face unless he'd just finished doing time.

"Ah, Detective." Jonesy snarled in response. "Why don't you mind your own business?"

"You're taking music lessons now?" O'Shea lifted the violin case from Jonesy's grasp. "I never thought of you as the artistic type."

"Thank God!" A voice rang out from behind the detective. "You caught him."

When O'Shea turned to see Aurora Lewis running toward him, Jonesy took his chance and made a break from the detective's grip.

"Shoot." O'Shea watched as the jailbird lit off down the sidewalk.

"Aren't you going to go after him?" asked Aurora, skidding to a stop.

"You should pay closer to attention to your belongings, Miss Lewis," said O'Shea, handing over the instrument. "What are you doing out after dark on a weeknight, anyway?"

She stammered for an answer. "Oh, you see, I have my embroidery class on Wednesdays after school." She paused. "Then a few of us got to talking afterward, and you know how girls are. We just can't keep track of time."

Detective O'Shea let her ramble on until she ran out of steam.

"You will go after that man, won't you?" she asked. "He shouldn't be allowed to just steal things from people."

"Don't worry. Jonesy's aiming to be picked up before the night's through. He's gotten used to sleeping in a warm place."

"Well, thank you, Detective O'Shea." Aurora patted the violin case. "You don't know what this means to me."

"I warned you about spending too much time with those young men from the Drama Academy, Miss Lewis," said the detective. "Stay clear of them and anything to do with your professor. That business is over and done with."

Aurora Lewis looked him straight in the eye. He could tell she believed his words as much as he did.

Chapter 23

WHEN AURORA LOOKED IN her bedroom mirror, she nearly didn't recognize herself. In her crisply pressed suit and polished black boots, along with a hint of blush and touch of lipstick, she could have walked into any fashionable event in the city. What a pity all her preparations were going to be wasted on a group of frumpy, middle-aged women eating watercress toasties and talking about their sciatica.

But at least Mother was happy that her daughter was showing more interest in ladylike activities. She was even allowing Aurora to wear silk stockings and had given her a small, beaded purse to carry her comb, hankie, and extra hair ribbon.

While dressing up was the fun part, Aurora still had a serious job to do at the luncheon. She reached into her jewelry box for her Maud Powell Society pin, giving the silver plating an extra polish before fastening it to her lapel. Then she took Miss Powell's red leather glove from her bottom dresser drawer and folded it neatly into her little handbag.

Aurora knew this would be her best chance to ask Miss Powell how her glove happened to be in Professor Schmieder's studio, although she wasn't going to bring it up quite like that. In fact, she didn't have a clue as to how she would manage to get some time alone with her.

She glanced at her closed closet door, behind which the professor's violin was safely hidden. Her teacher had always told her that being able to improvise was as important as reading notes on the page. Once she got to the museum, she would have to take his advice and come up with a plan on the spot.

"Aurora, are you ready?"

Her mother walked into the bedroom. She was dressed in a two-piece dark red walking suit accented by an enamel rose brooch.

"My, don't you look like a proper young lady?"

Aurora dropped into a slight curtsy. She was even starting to act more like a lady.

"Here, I brought something for you." Mother held out her loosely closed right hand. "Just to borrow, for today," she said. "Then for your next birthday, Father and I will buy you your own."

She opened her hand to reveal a pair of pearl earrings.

Aurora gasped.

"Oh, Mother. Didn't Father give these to you while you were engaged?"

"He most certainly did." Mother took her hand and gently laid the earrings into her palm. "And don't you dare lose them." She smiled. "Now let's see how they look on you."

Mother stood behind her, drawing her wavy red hair away from her face.

"You should wear your hair pinned back sometimes," she said. "You look much more mature."

Aurora gave a slight smile. After months of asking if she could wear her hair up, now Mother sounded like she had thought of the idea all on her own.

Taking the earrings one by one, her mother clipped them into place. For a moment they stood together looking in the mirror, and Aurora saw that in her mother's eyes she had been transformed into a young lady.

Mother gave her shoulders a light squeeze. But before Aurora had a chance to turn and give her a hug, Mother was walking back toward the bedroom door. The feeling of closeness had passed.

"Don't dawdle, Aurora. I don't want us to be the last ones to get there, after all the good tables are taken."

"Yes, Mother."

Blessed with the first truly sunny day in a week, Aurora suggested they leave the cab on the corner of Fifth Avenue and Eightieth Street and walk the last two blocks to the museum.

Since it was a school holiday, children were out playing ball and skipping rope on the sidewalk, braving the still-chilly temperatures but enjoying their few hours of freedom before heading back to their cramped apartments.

Aurora remembered how she and Grandmother used to walk to their favorite places in Central Park, where she could count the butterflies in spring and jump in the piles of leaves in autumn. Then as a special treat, after the first snowfall, the whole family would take a carriage to Pilgrim Hill. She and Father would charge to the top for their grand sled ride, while Grandmother and Mother cheered them on from the bottom of the slope.

But those delightful days lasted only for a few seasons. Father's back started bothering him, and Mother's attention turned to indoor amusements like shopping and ladies' lunches. The red sled was relegated to the storage room in the basement of the Osborne, and Aurora turned to her book-reading and daydreaming on winter afternoons.

"Aurora, let's speed up a little." Mother was already quickening her step as they turned onto the sidewalk leading to the museum entrance. "I think I see Mirabelle Stevens in front of us. She's the chairwoman for this luncheon, and I'd like to thank her for our invitation."

Set back from the avenue, the Metropolitan Museum of Art reminded Aurora of a sprawling Victorian mansion, absent the English countryside charm. With its dowdy redbrick walls, steep roofline, and arched windows that looked like a woman's raised eyebrows, the museum's architecture was considered so uninviting city residents had taken to calling it the Metropolitan Mausoleum.

"Hello there, Mirabelle." Mother waved with one hand while pulling Aurora along with the other. "Mirabelle, wait for me."

Mother didn't have to worry. Mrs. Stevens wasn't in any shape to move very fast. In fact, she was such a large woman that Aurora didn't see the slim blonde girl next to her until it was too late. In a second, Lucy left her mother's side to join her.

"Hello, Lucy," said Aurora.

"Gosh," said Lucy. "I'm surprised to see you here."

Much to Aurora's dismay, Lucy took her hand as they walked together.

"Good morning, Mrs. Lewis," Lucy said sweetly.

"Hello, dear," said Mother, but it was obvious her focus was on the elder of the Stevens pair. She hurried toward Mirabelle, leaving Aurora with her "little friend."

"I thought I'd be the only girl here my age," said Lucy.

"I asked my mother if I could come with her," said Aurora, "since I'm playing in Miss Powell's master class on Saturday."

"Then you must know all about her. Mother says Maud Powell is one of the best female violinists in the country."

"She's one of the best violinists, period," said Aurora. "Male or female."

"I think playing the violin for family and friends is fine," said Lucy, "but traveling all over the country and playing with men?" She shook her head. "I just don't think that's right."

Aurora didn't give in to her impulse to tug on one of Lucy's long blonde braids, although it wouldn't have done any good, anyway. Lucy was too simple of a girl to have real opinions of her own. Her mother had probably filled her head with talk about a woman's place being in the home. Aurora hoped Miss Powell wouldn't get any questions today about why she used her maiden name on stage, or when was she going to settle down to a nice, quiet family life. Why did a woman have to explain and reexplain herself when a man could just do what he wanted?

Walking through the museum entrance, the lobby wasn't much more appealing than the building's exterior, with its mottled marble floor and tall domed ceiling supported by metal beams. Mother, having paid her respects to Mrs. Stevens, was busy talking with two other women near the information desk. She motioned for Aurora to join her. Of course, Lucy decided to tag along.

"This is my daughter, Aurora," said her mother. "Aurora, these ladies are very dear friends of mine, Mrs. Wentworth and Mrs. Dodds."

"Very pleased to meet you." Aurora remembered something of her manners and curtsied slightly. Both of the women, who were years older than Mother, were wrapped in fur stoles and wore big diamond rings on their fingers.

"Aurora's playing her violin for Maud Powell in a master class on Saturday," said Mother. "That's why she's here with me today."

"Isn't that lovely?" said Mrs. Wentworth.

"How nice for you," said Mrs. Dodds.

End of conversation, as Aurora expected.

"Oh," said Mother. "This is Aurora's friend, Lucy Stevens. Mirabelle's daughter."

"My, my," said Mrs. Dodds. "Children grow up so fast these days. I remember when you were just a baby, Lucy. Now look at you, a lovely young lady and with such pretty blonde hair."

While Lucy and the ladies exchanged pleasantries, Aurora wandered over to the bulletin board listing the museum activities for the month. In the Antiquities Gallery, there was a new exhibit showcasing the latest artifacts from an expedition to Egypt, and there would be a talk given by the museum director on the Mastaba Tomb of Perneb. Aurora didn't know what it all meant but it sounded terribly exciting, and a little dangerous.

She felt a tap on her shoulder.

"Come along, Aurora," said Mother. "They're going to be starting soon."

She followed the women through the main corridor of the museum. Fortunately Lucy had gone up ahead with her own mother, so at least she wouldn't be bothered by her during the lunch.

They walked past medieval paintings lining the hallway and wide doorways leading to galleries waiting to be explored. Classics and French impressionists on the ground floor, Dutch old masters in the East Gallery upstairs, and American contemporaries in the West Gallery.

Aurora thought about abandoning her mission and instead losing herself in the treasures of the museum. But Theo and the boys were counting on her, and she'd already endured this much together time with Mother. She kept pace with the others and a few minutes later they entered the banquet room. The ladies were starting to select their seats at the tables, which were brightly decorated with white tablecloths and bouquets of fresh flowers. Maud Powell, dressed in a light blue suit, was standing at the front of the room, exchanging greetings with Mrs. Stevens. And Lucy Stevens was standing right next to her.

Aurora's jaw dropped. How could she have been so thickheaded? Mrs. Stevens was the chairwoman for the luncheon, and Miss Powell would naturally be seated at her table. If she had been friendlier with Lucy, she might have been invited to sit with them. Instead of Lucy, Aurora could have been chatting away with Miss Powell, finding just the right time to ask her about the professor.

"Aurora, dear. Over here."

Mother was sitting at the table with those fussbudgets she'd been talking to in the museum lobby. Before taking her seat with them,

Aurora looked again toward the front table. As if she knew she was being watched, Lucy raised her chin a bit and smiled even wider.

Aurora plopped down in her chair. However entertaining a conversation Lucy and Miss Powell were having, she couldn't imagine comparing it to Mrs. Dodds's fascinating description of the color of her azaleas in full bloom.

After several attempts by Mrs. Stevens to quiet the crowd's applause, she finally drew an end to the ladies' club monthly luncheon.

"Thank you so much, Miss Powell, for sharing your inspirational story with us. And for talking about how each of us can encourage our daughters to reach for their dreams." Mrs. Stevens dabbed the corner of her eye with a handkerchief. "I know we will all remember your talk for a long time to come."

For Aurora, truer words couldn't have been spoken. From recounting her humble beginnings in a small town in Illinois to her pioneering performance at the 1893 World Exposition in Chicago, Miss Powell's message was clear. Even though women still couldn't vote in this country and weren't allowed to audition for professional orchestras, they needed to keep working toward achieving their goals, whether that be teaching at a large university, heading their own company, or becoming a violin soloist.

Revolutionary talk for a group of women whose main concern was usually what was on the evening menu. But Miss Powell, primly dressed and ever gracious, made her case not with fire and fury, but with simple language and by using her own life as an example.

"Let's go and meet her," said Mother, pointing to the queue of well-wishers already forming in front of Miss Powell's table. "I want her to know you're playing in her class."

Aurora nearly pinched herself to make sure she wasn't dreaming. Mother had never shown interest in anything to do with her music studies.

Stepping in front of Aurora when they reached the head of the line, Mother offered her congratulations to Miss Powell.

"Your speech was marvelous," she said. "The best we've ever had in this club."

"Thank you. I'm glad you liked it," said Miss Powell.

"I'm Mrs. Lewis. Mrs. Marguerite Lewis."

Aurora nudged her mother, in case she'd forgotten she was standing right behind her.

"Oh, yes," said Mother, moving to the side. "This is my daughter, Aurora. She also enjoyed your talk very much."

Miss Powell first looked at the shiny Maud Powell club pin on Aurora's collar and then at her face.

"Have we met before?" she asked.

"Yes," said Aurora, surprised that she remembered. "At the Philharmonic concert last Sunday."

Miss Powell drew a blank look.

Mother leaned into the conversation.

"Aurora is a violinist, too. A very fine one."

"That's right," said Miss Powell, the memory finally registering. "You're going to be in my master class. Didn't you tell me what piece you're playing?"

"Maud, dear, there's someone here you must meet." Mrs. Stevens stepped between Aurora and Miss Powell. "Dr. Robinson, over here."

A slender, pale man came forward.

"Good afternoon, Madame," he said. "I'm the director of the museum. It's such a pleasure to meet you."

A museum director took precedence over a high school girl any day. Just like that, Aurora's conversation with Miss Powell was over.

After saying their good-byes to Mrs. Wentworth and Mrs. Dodds, Aurora and her mother left the banquet room. Lucy Stevens joined them, full of details about her lunch with their guest speaker, going on and on about Miss Powell's preference for chicken instead of beef and how she drank her tea with milk just like an English lady.

Lucy's incessant chattering only made Aurora feel worse. She'd spent the whole afternoon without having any kind of meaningful conversation with Miss Powell. She couldn't leave without at least trying to get a few words alone with her.

"Mother, I need to go back," she said.

"What is it now?" asked Mother, hardly slowing down her step.

It was the time for some improvising.

"I forgot my hair ribbon. I took it out of my purse because I thought I would tie my hair back during lunch. I think I left it on the table."

Mother stopped in front of one the suits of armor on display. The resemblance was uncanny, but Aurora held back any comment.

"I'll only be a minute," she said instead.

"Are you sure left it?" her mother asked. "I didn't see anything on the table."

"Positive." Aurora was already on her way. "You keep going. I'll catch up with you in the lobby."

"Wait," said Lucy. "I'll come with you."

"No," said Aurora, sounding harsher than she intended. "I'll see you next week at school."

For a moment, it looked like Lucy might break into tears. Aurora felt sorry for speaking so sharply, but she would make it up to her somehow.

The last of the luncheon attendees, with Mrs. Stevens leading the way, were walking down the hallway. Only Miss Powell wasn't among them. Aurora walked faster. How could she have missed her?

When she reached the banquet room, her heart sank. The waitstaff was already clearing off the tables and having a good time of it, too. The younger boys snapped linen napkins at each other, while the older fellows whistled after the girls on the crew. Aurora slipped away, leaving them to their fun and games.

Downcast, and in no hurry to find her mother, Aurora took the long way back to the lobby. Two turns past the white marble sculptures in the Ancient Greece collection, she was in the gallery of color and light. On the far wall hung one of her favorite paintings, Renoir's *Madame Charpentier and Her Children*.

Aurora was heartened to see she wasn't the only one who admired the artist's scene of a mother with her two curly-haired daughters and their big, fluffy dog. A woman in a light blue suit was standing before the painting, studying it carefully.

"Hello again," Aurora said quietly, walking up to her.

Miss Powell gave a small jump.

"Goodness." She put her hand to her chest. "You startled me. Are you a fan of the French impressionists, too?"

"Yes, ma'am." Aurora moved nearer to the painting. "I love the way the dog is just lying there, not paying any attention to the little girls playing around him."

"You know, this work was very controversial in its day," said Miss Powell. "It was the museum's first impressionist painting, and the board almost fired the curator because it was too modern. Just a few years later, it seems very familiar."

Miss Powell paused for a moment. Here was Aurora's chance.

"Mother and I really enjoyed your talk today," she said.

"I'm glad. This group was so easy to speak to. Sometimes at these women's clubs, the reception isn't so inviting."

Aurora opened her purse. "After the lecture, I wanted to ask you something."

"Did you want my autograph?" asked Miss Powell. "I'd be happy to sign another one for you."

"No, it's not that," said Aurora. "I think I may have something of yours." She took the red glove out of her handbag.

"Why, what's this?" Miss Powell's face brightened. "I've been looking all over for these. I couldn't remember the last time I was wearing …"

She drew a sharp breath. It was as good as a confirmation for Aurora.

Miss Powell took the glove from her, running her finger over the finely stitched monogram of her first initial.

"You said you were a student of Anton Schmieder's?" she asked.

"Yes, ma'am."

"Was he a good teacher?"

"I thought so."

The two fell silent. Aurora felt as if she had intruded on a private memory. She couldn't bring herself to ask how the glove had ended up in the professor's studio on the day he died.

"Where's the other one?" Miss Powell spoke at last.

Aurora thought she hadn't heard her correctly.

"The other glove," said Miss Powell. "They usually come in pairs, don't they?"

Whatever moment of reflection that had occurred was over. Miss Powell was all business now.

Aurora hesitated.

"We—I mean, I thought you only dropped this one."

"No, I lost both of them." Miss Powell handed the glove back to her. "Here, keep it. I can't very well wear one without the other."

She spun on her heel and headed for the gallery exit.

With nothing to lose, Aurora blurted out the question she'd been intending to ask all along.

"Why were you in Professor Schmieder's studio Saturday morning?"

Miss Powell stiffened but kept on walking.

Aurora gave it another try.

"What were you two arguing about? What made you so angry with him?"

Miss Powell turned to face her. Aurora expected to hear a litany of cross words, but instead she sighed, looking more sad than upset.

"Some things, Aurora, are better left not knowing."

Chapter 24

Detective O'Shea took another sip from his now cold cup of coffee, which had been none too warm to start with, all the while keeping his eyes fixed on the street entrance to Finkelstein's club. Seated at a window booth in the coffee shop across the avenue, O'Shea had seen customers arrive by automobile, trolley, and on foot. Even on a Thursday night, the place was packing them in.

He got himself comfortable, watching and waiting, although he didn't know for what exactly. Except that the big-eared kid showing up at both the club and the professor's studio made him curious.

"Can I get you a piece of pie?" asked the shop's waitress. "We've got blueberry, and it's still pretty fresh."

"No, thanks," said O'Shea. "But could you warm up my coffee?"

He slid his cup toward the edge of the table.

"You been working here long?" he asked, still keeping tabs on the activity across the street. It didn't hurt to start up a little conversation to help pass the time.

"Been working here long enough," she said. "Nearly three months."

"Tough being on the late shift, ain't it?" asked O'Shea.

"Today I'm working a double," she said. "But at least I'll get home in time for a few hours sleep before my boy gets up for school in the morning."

"Why can't your husband take care of him?" he asked. "That way you could sleep in."

"You're funny, mister. Why do you think I'm working so much? There's no husband around to take care of us."

She probably wasn't older than twenty or twenty-one, but her tired eyes and stooped shoulders added years to her looks. She might have had nice brown hair once, but now it was all wiry and broken off at the ends. He felt guilty sitting there while she waited on him, when she was the one whose feet were aching from standing all day.

"Why don't you join me?" He nodded toward the seat opposite him. "Take a load off."

"I can't." She glanced at the door to the kitchen. "Frank will fire me if he catches me taking a break. And I really need this job."

She began to move away. "I should start some of my cleanup, if you're not going to order anything else."

"Then go ahead and bring me a piece of that blueberry pie," said O'Shea. "A fat guy like me can always eat one more piece of pie."

The waitress smiled. Behind her worn-out expression, she might have passed for pretty.

"You're not so fat," she said. "You should see some of the fellas that come in here."

A bald-headed man with mean black eyes stuck his head out from behind the kitchen door.

"Gayla," he said, in a low, menacing tone.

"Right there, Frank." The waitress stood up straight but gave a wink to the detective.

"I'll get you that piece of pie, sir," she said, in a louder than normal tone of voice. Then she said softly, "An extra big slice."

O'Shea chuckled as he turned his attention back to the club scene. Or what was left of it. Most of the patrons were already inside, probably lined up on those rickety steps waiting to get into the show five floors up. The sidewalk was nearly deserted, except for a couple standing under the street lamp. He recognized the girl as the stringbean waitress who had been his server at the club the other night. What was her name again? Maribel, or was it Miriam? Yeah, that was it.

Miriam stood facing in O'Shea's direction, stamping her feet and pulling a thin shawl around her shoulders as meager protection from the cold. Her male companion, whose back was to the detective, was wearing a winter jacket and wool cap. What kind of louse would let his girlfriend freeze while he stood there nice and warm?

The man was waving his arms and pointing at Miriam. Although O'Shea couldn't hear the words being exchanged, from Miriam's scared expression he could tell it was more of an argument than a conversation. A one-way argument that the man was winning.

Then Miriam made the mistake of pushing the agitated fellow's hand away from her face. He stepped in closer and a second later, his right fist caught Miriam on the chin. She fell backward onto the pavement. As she lay there, the guy threw something at her.

Detective O'Shea wriggled out of the booth, nearly knocking over the waitress who was coming back from the kitchen with a big piece of pie with ice cream on top.

"What about your order?" she asked, but O'Shea was already out the door.

"How could you lose it?" The detective could hear the man shouting at Miriam. "You know I need that money."

Then he grabbed her hair and pulled her head back.

"Hey, you punk," yelled O'Shea, starting to cross the street. "What do you think you're doing? Leave that girl alone."

The fellow dropped his grip on Miriam and turned around. That's when the detective saw his face. The bully was no man; he was the kid who worked in the club. Aurora Lewis's accuser.

A motor car speeding down the road sent the detective back to the curb. By the time he finally got across the street, he could see the kid running away.

"Just wait until the next time I catch you." O'Shea shook his fist at him. "Let's see you mess with somebody who can fight back."

As for the victim in the quarrel, Miriam was nowhere to be seen. She would probably be too afraid to file a complaint, but O'Shea wanted to at least make sure she was all right.

"Darn girls." He leaned on the light pole to catch his breath. "When will they ever learn to stay away from those lowlifes?"

Looking down, he saw what Miriam's boyfriend had thrown at her. In her rush to get away, she'd left it on the sidewalk.

It was a glove.

The detective picked it up. At least it was made of good leather, not the cheap stuff. Unusual red color, too.

He wondered how Miriam was able to afford something this nice on the starvation wages Abe Finkelstein must be paying her. And it didn't look like her boyfriend was the kind of guy to give her any expensive presents.

Detective O'Shea stuffed the glove into his pocket. Maybe he'd have a chance to give it back to Miriam someday. Or if she was watching from some hiding place, she would get up the courage to find him and ask for it. Then he would tell her a thing or two about how to get rid of that bad-news boyfriend.

"Yoo-hoo."

The detective looked around to see who was calling him.

"I'm over here."

The woman's voice was coming from across the street. The waitress was standing in the doorway of the coffee shop, still holding his piece of pie. Now that's what he called service.

Chapter 25

IF THERE IS A God, he must live in the New York Public Library.

Aurora looked up in wonder at the fluffy white clouds floating along the high blue ceiling of the Rose Main Reading Room.

"It's like we're in heaven," she whispered.

"Maybe we are," Theo whispered back.

The room stretched out before them with rows and rows of long oak tables. Even though Aurora and the boys had gotten there just as the library opened on Friday morning, every seat was already taken. But the great hall was completely quiet except for the rustling of papers or the soft-heeled footsteps of a page delivering books to another voracious reader.

"This must be what smart folks do during the day," said Eddie.

Bill came walking down the aisle toward them.

"There aren't any places to sit," he said, keeping his voice down. "Besides, I don't think they like people talking in here. Let's go back to the landing."

They retreated to the third-floor vestibule and found an empty bench on the far side of the rotunda-shaped space. Here they were surrounded by statues of literary figures like Nietzsche and Tolstoy, and quotations from the great works of Shakespeare and Dickens were inscribed on the walls of white stone.

"I love coming to this place," said Aurora. "Especially seeing those lions guarding the entrance."

"It is quite an achievement," said Theo, pointing to the vaulted ceiling and stained-glass windows. "No building in the city quite matches it.

The library director is a brilliant man who sketched out the design on a piece of scrap paper."

"Ahem, Theo," said Eddie. "Maybe we could get the history lesson another time. We came to hear about what happened when Aurora met Maud Powell, remember?"

Theo nodded with a smile. "You're right. Aurora, why don't you tell us what you found out?"

Aurora replayed the tale of her odd encounter with Miss Powell at the museum, confirming that the glove was hers, along with her cryptic parting words about "better not knowing."

"What did you do after she said that?" asked Theo.

"A group of noisy school kids came into the room and I got distracted. When I turned around, Miss Powell wasn't there. She must have gone to another gallery or upstairs. I didn't see her in the lobby when we were leaving."

"If there's something better not to know, that means there's something more to know," said Theo.

"Perhaps we should pay Miss Powell a visit," said Bill. "As it turns out, I happen to know the hotel where she's staying."

Three sets of eyes turned toward him.

"You mean you've known all this time and didn't say anything to us?" asked Eddie.

"Not really," said Bill. "But as you like to remind me, I do enjoy frequenting the finer restaurants in town. Last night I had a delicious tenderloin at the Round Table in the Algonquin Hotel. And guess who happened to be sitting right next to me? Miss Powell and her husband, or Mr. and Mrs. Turner, as the *maître d'* called them. When they got up to leave, Mr. Turner told him to charge the dinner to their room, number 512."

"Bill, I'm never going to kid you again about your expensive tastes," said Theo. "Knights and Lady of the Round Table." He stood up and gave a bow to Aurora. "We're off to the Algonquin."

Chapter 26

"My wife isn't accepting visitors right now, Detective. Perhaps you can see her another time when we're in the city."

Godfrey Turner's attempt to close the door of room 512 in the Algonquin Hotel was blocked by Barney O'Shea's big right foot.

"I'm just checking to see if everything is all right with her violin, Mr. Turner," said the detective. "I used to work security down at Carnegie Hall, and I know how the musicians can get attached to their instruments."

"Who's there, Godfrey?" A woman called out from behind the door. "Is the maid back with my laundry? I just phoned down to the front desk to find out what's keeping her."

Godfrey didn't answer.

"Ah, Mrs. Turner?" O'Shea raised his voice so she could hear him. "This is Detective O'Shea, from the New York City Police Department. We met briefly the other day, backstage at Carnegie Hall."

"You mean you've talked to my wife before?" asked Mr. Turner. "She didn't tell me anything about that."

Maud Powell appeared behind her husband in the doorway.

"For heaven's sake, Godfrey. Let the man in before the whole hotel gets an earful."

Godfrey reluctantly stepped aside to allow O'Shea into the room.

"What's this all about, Maud?" he asked, shutting the door behind the detective. "Why on earth do the police want to talk to you?"

Maud ignored her husband.

"Won't you have a seat, Detective?"

She ushered him into the sitting room of the hotel suite, although it looked more like a fancy apartment to Detective O'Shea, what with the plush furniture and silver tea service laid out on the sideboard. A glowing fire in the fireplace kept the room comfortably warm. Guess the music business paid off for some folks, while others, like Professor Schmieder, could barely make a living.

"What is it you want this time, Detective?" she asked once they were settled into the overstuffed brocade chairs.

"I wanted to see if everything was okay with your violin," repeated O'Shea. "I heard your office got a real going-over, Mr. Turner."

Godfrey nodded. "It took my secretary all day to put everything back to normal."

"And your violin didn't suffer any damage, Mrs. Turner?" asked O'Shea.

"Not a bit," said Maud. "It's survived floods and fires; a couple of clumsy burglars weren't about to hurt it."

"Any news on catching the guys who broke in?" asked Godfrey.

"The department is doing everything they can, sir," said O'Shea.

No one talked for a few awkward moments.

"Is there anything else, Detective?" Maud asked at last.

"Just more thing," he said. "I've been doing a little more checking on the music teacher I told you about, Anton Schmieder."

"Schmieder?" asked Godfrey. "You mean the old gent who fell out the window over at the Towers? I heard about the accident earlier this week. But what's he got to do with my wife?"

"You mean you haven't told him?" O'Shea asked Maud, but she didn't look in his direction.

"That's why I went to see your wife at Carnegie Hall, Mr. Turner," he said. "It's not a secret that she was an acquaintance of the late professor. No use denying it, Mrs. Turner."

Maud shrugged. "I studied with him when I attended the Heidelberg Conservatory. That was many years ago."

Godfrey fidgeted in his chair but kept quiet.

"And was that the last time you saw him?" asked O'Shea.

Maud winced at the question.

"I imagine the orchestra players couldn't keep their mouths shut," she said, standing up to warm her hands by the fire. "No, I saw Anton just a few days ago."

"Could you be more specific?" asked the detective.

"Before the Philharmonic concert on Friday. Anton came backstage to see me and wish me good luck on the performance."

"Is that so? Would you say it was a friendly reunion?"

Godfrey Turner glared at O'Shea.

"Look here, Detective. You're not going to waste our time on some kind of fishing expedition. Come out and say what you're looking for."

"Take it easy, Mr. Turner. I have reason to believe your wife is not telling me the whole story about her relationship with Anton Schmieder." O'Shea paused. "Now Mrs. Turner, why don't we start over, and you tell me the real reason he came backstage to see you on Friday night."

Maud crossed the room and sat down on the ottoman at her husband's feet.

"There's not much mystery about what he wanted from me. I'm sure our voices were loud enough for at least half the orchestra to hear." She leaned back against Godfrey's knee. "It's more of a tragedy, really. Anton Schmieder was a broken man, looking for a quick handout to get him through the next few days."

"I suppose you turned him down when he asked you for the money," said O'Shea.

"Of course she did," said Godfrey. "We're not running a charity here. Maud gets requests like this all the time. If she helped everyone who asked her, we'd be the ones in the poorhouse."

"Godfrey, really," said Maud. "You make it sound worse than it is."

The detective took a long look at the famous violinist before asking his next question.

"When did you really see the professor for the last time, Mrs. Turner?"

She looked back at him with the same, unwavering gaze.

"You already know the answer to that, don't you, Detective?"

O'Shea nodded. "Yes, ma'am. I believe I do."

Aurora and the boys casually walked through the black-and-gold covered entrance of the Algonquin Hotel, trying not to draw attention to themselves. The cozy lobby gave an intimate feel to the place, with leather-trimmed wing chairs arranged among the mahogany writing desks and low end tables. The floor was covered in a deep-blue patterned rug, complementing the dark woodwork and carved pillars extending up to the white ceiling.

Hotel guests were mingling in groups of twos and threes, planning their day's excursion or taking advantage of the always-open refreshment bar just off the lobby.

"Let's go over there," said Theo, nodding to a couch and chair near the window looking onto Forty-Fourth Street. "Then we can decide what we want to do."

"I could go up to Miss Powell's room," said Bill once they were seated. "I'll say I'm with room service and then get in to talk to her."

"Talk to her about what?" asked Theo. "Even if you could get that far, she'll deny knowing anything. I say we wait here for a while and see if she goes anywhere. Then we can follow her."

"All of us?" asked Eddie. "That would look mighty strange."

Aurora thought the same thing, but she didn't want to put down Theo's idea in front of the other fellows.

"Whatever we decide to do, we can't hang out here indefinitely," said Bill. "The guy behind the reception desk is already giving us the evil stare."

Sure enough, the hotel clerk was keeping his focus on them, until a delivery man with a red cap distracted his attention.

"There's something about that guy I don't like," said Eddie.

Theo glanced at the front desk.

"The hotel clerk? Forget about him. Now who's got a better plan for how we should approach Miss Powell?"

"Not the clerk," said Eddie. "It's the delivery guy I don't like. And I know why." He stood up. "Wait a second, you over there," he called out.

A dozen people in the lobby looked toward him, everyone except the fellow he was talking to.

"Bill, guard the front door," said Eddie.

Without asking why, Bill sprang out of his chair and moved into place.

The delivery guy finally turned around. But he was just an overgrown kid with big ears.

Eddie high-hurtled over an arm chair, but the kid was too quick. He skirted away as Eddie tumbled head over heels into the registration desk.

With Bill stationed at the front entrance, the young fellow took off in the opposite direction. Theo was the next one with a chance to grab him. But after a crisscross chase around the stunned hotel guests, he slipped on one of the throw rugs and ended up facedown on the floor. Aurora ran over to check on him while the hooligan dashed into an adjoining hallway and out of sight.

Just then the elevator doors opened, depositing guests from the upper floors straight into the confusion. One of the passengers was a hefty man wearing a police badge.

"Oh, great," Aurora said to herself. Detective O'Shea couldn't have shown up at a worse time.

"What's going on around here?" bellowed the detective.

The desk clerk was immediately at his side.

"Officer, you need to arrest this gang of troublemakers. They're causing a riot in here. This is a respectable place, I'll have you know."

What a gang, thought Aurora. Theo was slow getting to his feet, and Eddie was still trying to get his bearings. Bill, on the other hand, was his usual unruffled self.

O'Shea surveyed the situation without saying anything. But he shook his head when he saw Aurora standing in the middle of the mayhem.

"Excitement's over, folks." He spoke in a calming voice to the hotel patrons. "Go on about your business. Sorry for the disruption." He turned to the clerk. "You too. I'll take care of this. You don't need to worry about it."

"But it happened on my shift," said the man.

"Have your manager call me if there are any problems," said the detective. "Barney O'Shea. He knows me."

The clerk resumed his post, still mumbling under his breath.

Detective O'Shea walked over to Theo and spoke in a low voice. "I want to see you and your friends down at the station. I'll be back there after lunch. If you don't come in, I'll have you all picked up." He gestured toward Aurora. "Including the girl."

Chapter 27

BEING THAT IT WAS her first time in a police station, Aurora had expected the place to be bustling with cops and captured robbers. But the midtown precinct was hardly a hotbed of criminal activity. The most exciting thing going on was an elderly lady complaining to the officer behind the desk about a cat stuck on the ledge outside her apartment window, meowing day and night. Why couldn't a policeman come out and do something about it, she wanted to know.

"Tough old gal, isn't she?" said Bill as they waited behind her.

"Not so loud," said Aurora. "She'll hear you."

"They could do something about all the pigeons, too, while they're at it," said Eddie, not bothering to keep his voice down. "Those birds are an awful nuisance, making a mess all over the city."

"They're actually very intelligent animals," said Theo. "Pigeons have been used as couriers ever since ancient Egyptian times."

"They can all fly back there as far as I'm concerned," said Eddie.

"Try putting out a saucer of milk for the nice kitty." The desk attendant gestured for Granny to move along, even though she was still going on about the crying cat.

"Next," said the officer.

Theo stepped up.

"We're here to see Detective O'Shea," he said.

The desk man gave them a long look.

"All of you?"

"Yes, all of us," said Theo. "He told us to come in here."

"Okay, you sign in for the bunch." The officer slid the log-in sheet toward him. "But you'll have to take a seat until he can see you." He pointed to the waiting area. "I'll let you know when he's ready."

Twenty minutes later, they were still sitting there. The desk officer hadn't even called to see if the detective could talk to them. He was too busy reading some kind of training manual and making a few notes to himself in the margins.

"This is ridiculous," said Eddie. "O'Shea told us to come in, and now he won't even see us."

He got up to leave.

"No," said Theo, holding on to Eddie's arm. "Wait a minute."

A policeman was leading a small group of detainees through the double doors that led to the precinct's back rooms. But these weren't your typical lawbreakers; they were middle-class women, and a few men, carrying handmade signs with slogans like "We'll fight until we win" and "Clothing workers unite."

"Another rally gone amok," said Bill. "You can't walk down the street these days without running into a demonstration about something or other."

Theo nodded as the last of the protestors shuffled through the doorway.

"Let's follow them," he said in a hushed voice.

"What?" asked Aurora.

Before she got an answer, the boys were out of their chairs and headed for the door. Aurora glanced at the desk attendant, but he was studying his handbook even more intently, paying no attention to them.

She'd never heard of sneaking *into* a police station. But she'd better hurry if she didn't want to be left behind.

The back office was nearly empty except for a few patrolmen who barely looked their way. The protestors were nowhere to be seen.

"There's Detective O'Shea," said Theo, pointing to the other side of the room.

Sitting behind a cheap wooden desk, the detective was tipped back in his chair with his feet propped up on an upside-down trash can. His eyes were closed, his jaw hanging open.

"Pride of the department," said Bill as they drew closer. "Hard at work."

A younger policeman who Aurora recognized from the professor's studio came forward to block their path.

"What are you doing back here?" he asked. "Who let you in?"

"We're here to see Detective O'Shea," said Theo, nodding at the sleeping giant.

"Wait a second, I know who you are," said the officer. "You're those students from the Carnegie Towers. But that violin teacher case is closed."

"Even so," said Theo. "The detective told us to come in."

The officer studied him for a moment and then turned and started banging his fist on O'Shea's desk.

"Stop snoozing, Barney."

The detective stirred.

"What's going on, Daley?" he asked.

"You've got some visitors," said the sergeant.

O'Shea took his time sitting up in his chair.

"So you came in after all," he said.

"That's what you wanted, right?" asked Theo. "What's the idea of treating us like a bunch of delinquents?"

The detective pursed his lips.

"I've seen my share of delinquents, and you, Mr. Eckstein, don't even make the list. But your buddy here, he's another story." O'Shea pointed to Eddie. "Picking locks comes second nature to boys from his neighborhood. Don't it, Mr. Goldenberg?"

Eddie squirmed in place but kept his mouth shut.

The detective looked at Bill.

"And your fancy friend here has enough IOUs piled up around town to make life interesting," he said. "As for Miss Lewis, she always seems to show up in the most peculiar places. In the music studio of a dead man, a cabaret club blocks from home, and in a disturbance in a nice hotel."

Aurora looked at him with a start. How did he know about her being at Finkelstein's?

"Miss Lewis, you forgot what I told you," O'Shea said solemnly. "Be smart and mind your mother and stay away from these boys if you know what's good for you."

He reached into his desk and pulled out his police revolver, letting it rest in his hand so they all could get a good look.

"As for you three numbskulls, if I catch you even crossing the street the wrong way, I'll have you locked up faster than you can say 'Willy Shakespeare.'"

He placed the revolver in his hip holster.

"Now get out of here. I've got work to do." With a wave of his hand, he shooed them away from the desk.

"What was that all about?" asked Aurora, once they reached the sidewalk outside the station. "First he tells us to come over here, and then he can't wait to get rid of us."

"O'Shea is trying to scare us off," said Theo. "He knows we're on to something about Professor Schmieder and he's thinking the same way. Otherwise, he wouldn't have been in Maud Powell's hotel today."

"But what about the delivery kid?" asked Eddie. "Why'd he end up at the hotel too?"

No one could answer that question.

"The main thing is O'Shea doesn't think Aurora had anything to do with the professor's death," said Theo. "Otherwise he wouldn't be following these other leads." He turned to Aurora. "But now the most important thing for you to do is to practice for tomorrow's master class. We're all going to be there."

Aurora was surprised they'd even remembered, what with their busy school schedules and everything else that had happened this week.

"You'd do that for me?" she asked. "I mean, all of you will come?"

"Of course. We can't wait to hear you," said Theo, although Eddie and Bill didn't look as enthusiastic. "Polish up on your violin so you can impress Miss Powell."

She smiled halfheartedly at his reference to "your" violin, but she wasn't going to say anything about the mix-up with Professor Schmieder's while they were standing in front of a police station.

"I'll try to play my best," she said. "See you all tomorrow."

Detective O'Shea grimaced as he leaned back in his chair. Hopefully his tough talk with those kids would keep them out of his way and out of any more trouble. He was convinced that whoever was responsible for the professor's death wouldn't think twice about getting rid of anyone who got too close to the truth.

"Hey, Daley," he said. "I never got a chance to ask you if you found that violin again in the music teacher's studio."

"I'm tired of you sending me on these wild-goose chases," said Daley. "I didn't find any violin this time. And the place has been locked up tight, I checked with the building manager before I left."

"You don't say," said O'Shea, putting his feet back up on the trash can. "You don't say."

Chapter 28

THE COLD WINTER SUN had barely risen above the Seventh Avenue skyline by the time Aurora woke up on Saturday morning. With frost covering her bedroom window, she spent another hour lying beneath the warm covers, thinking about all that was ahead of her. The day she had prepared for was finally here, the master class with Miss Powell on the stage of Carnegie Hall.

She ran through the schedule in her mind. She would arrive backstage with plenty of time to warm up. At eleven o'clock the class would start, and she would sit politely listening to the other participants. When her name was called she would take a deep breath, walk to the center of the stage, bow to the applause of the audience, and then turn toward Miss Powell. She would lift the violin to her shoulder, check the tension in the bow, close her eyes, and begin.

It was all so heavenly. Aurora could already hear the music of the Paganini "Romanze" in her head. Her family would be in the audience, proud of her accomplishment. Theo, Bill, and Eddie would be there, too, listening to Miss Powell congratulate her on her playing.

Only Professor Schmieder would be missing. Maybe it was a sign that she had ended up with his violin after all, playing one of his favorite pieces. What could be a more fitting tribute to her teacher?

Aurora opened her eyes and sat up. It was already nine o'clock. Time to get ready.

Rolling out of bed was never Barney O'Shea's strong suit. But the alarm going off at nine this morning was downright painful, seeing how he'd gotten back to his room in the boardinghouse only a few hours earlier. He'd been pulled into an armed robbery action over on Eighth Avenue just before getting off work at midnight. The train station office had been held-up as the night clerks counted the daily receipts, and with the robbers still holed up inside, every able-bodied officer in the vicinity had been called over to lock down the perimeter. Turned out that the job's ringleader, a big, ugly guy with an "I love Mama" tattoo on his right arm, decided to give himself up without a fight. After they'd waited around for hours in the cold.

O'Shea threw a quick splash of water on his face. He was going to a music concert at Carnegie Hall this morning, the one where Aurora Lewis would be playing for Maud Powell. Seeing as how they would be near the place where Professor Schmieder died, O'Shea figured it wouldn't hurt to keep an eye on the two ladies who probably knew him best. He'd also given Sergeant Daley a heads-up to be in the area around eleven. The sergeant grumbled like always, but O'Shea wanted him nearby in case some less than desirable characters associated with the professor decided to make an appearance.

On his way out, he picked up his revolver from the dresser and tucked it into his holster. No harm in having a little extra insurance.

"I don't know about this," said Eddie as he, Bill, and Theo sat in the corner booth at Rosenberg's waiting for their flapjacks and eggs. "Except for Aurora, listening to a bunch of violinists doesn't sound like a fun way to spend a Saturday morning. I was thinking of going down to the harbor to watch the RMS *Olympic* come into port. She'll be the biggest ocean liner to come to New York until the *Titanic* sails here next year."

"Before you volunteered us for this musical snoozefest, I had an appointment with my tailor," said Bill. "Isn't there any way we could just see Aurora's part and then leave?"

"You saw how her face lit up when I told her we were going to be there," said Theo. "Besides, I just want to be sure." His voice trailed off.

"Sure about what?" asked Bill.

"It's nothing," said Theo.

"Are you expecting something other than a couple hours of captivating violin music?" asked Bill.

"Yeah, Theo," said Eddie. "What are you thinking?"

"I just want us to be there, that's all," he said. "It's only been a week since Professor Schmieder fell out the window. Whoever is responsible is still out there."

"You don't think that somebody would try to hurt Aurora, do you?" asked Eddie.

Before Theo could answer, their waitress was at the table, balancing three steaming plates of flapjacks in two hands.

"Here you go, gents." Delores unceremoniously slid the plates down in front of them. "I'll be back with the rest of your order."

"Oh, miss." Bill raised his coffee cup. "I could use a freshening up."

Delores rolled her eyes. "Must be my lucky day."

Chapter 29

Dressed in her new recital outfit, a white linen dress with a dark green sash, Aurora took a last bite of crumb cake and sip of hot chocolate. Her family would walk over to Carnegie Hall just before the master class started, but she needed to get going.

She kissed Mother and Grandmother good-bye as they finished their coffee at the dining table.

"Be careful on the sidewalk, Aurora," said her mother. "It's icy out there this morning."

"I will, Mother," she said. "Grandmother, will you be able to make it?"

Her grandmother nodded. "Don't worry. I wouldn't miss a single note."

Then Aurora waved to her father, who was sitting in the parlor reading the newspaper.

"Aurora, wait a minute," he called out as she was putting on her coat.

That was odd, she thought. Father never spoke much around the house, especially when he was reading the paper.

"What is it?" she asked, taking up the violin case she had set out by the front door earlier that morning. The case holding Professor Schmieder's violin.

"Come here for a minute," said her father.

Aurora walked back toward the parlor, curious about what was so important.

"There's an article in here about a break-in at a music promoter's office downtown," said Father. "The thieves were looking for a violin but got scared away at the last minute. Also says here that another violin was taken from the opera house not too long ago, and the police think both incidents could be connected to a burglary ring in the city." He looked up at her. "Better keep a good eye on yours, Aurora," he said. "We don't want it to be next."

Aurora's grip tightened around the handle of the violin case, thinking back to her run-in with the robber on the street a couple nights ago. But he didn't look like he was part of a conspiracy of thieves. According to Detective O'Shea, Jonesy was a petty con man who was willing to get caught if it meant a warm bed on a cold night.

"Don't worry, Father," she said. "I'll see you over at the hall soon."

Leaving the apartment, she wondered how long she'd be able to keep up the charade with the switched violins. But at least this morning the professor's would be safely in her care. Now she needed to think about her performance. She reminded herself that even though she knew the music by heart, Professor Schmieder always said that on concert day the best preparation was to take the time to reawaken your senses and steady your nerves.

But when she arrived backstage at Carnegie Hall, she realized she wasn't the only performer with that idea. Not even the second or third, considering the endless cascade of notes coming from the behind the greenroom door.

As much as Aurora had been looking forward to this day, she was now as much afraid. She'd given little thought to the four other players in the master class, each of whom would be just as keen to draw Miss Powell's praise and attention.

Even her choice of music seemed all wrong. The Paganini was a lyrical piece with long, sweeping melodic lines, lovely to listen to but no match for the brilliance of the Vieuxtemps and Wieniawski selections she was hearing. Professor Schmieder believed that a well-turned phrase was worth more than a page of black notes. But she was starting to think her teacher's advice was out-of-date with current musical tastes and its emphasis on flash and technique.

"Are you going in?"

A tall young woman with sleek black hair was standing behind her. She was carrying a violin case and wearing a dark blue fitted bodice and skirt. Aurora, in her girlish white dress with the big green bow, felt even more out of place.

"Are you going in?" the woman asked again.

Aurora stepped back to let her through. Just inside the door she could see a young man wearing a gray suit, playing his violin and swaying to the music. Two more violinists watched as the woman in blue entered but continued on with their practicing without skipping a beat.

There was no way Aurora could go in now. Perhaps Professor Schmieder could have convinced her that she had as much right to be there as anyone else. Maybe even more, what with all that she'd gone through to get this far. Instead, she gave herself an excuse. If she did join the others, she wouldn't be able to hear her own playing, anyway. So she turned and walked away.

Where could she go for a few minutes to collect herself? Then she thought of the Carnegie Towers. She could find an out-of-the-way spot upstairs to practice and still be back in plenty of time to join the others on stage for the start of the class.

Entering the lobby, she saw the elevator doors standing open and Maurice the operator waiting at attention for his next customer. Aurora stepped into the iron box and asked to go up to the fourth floor. With a quick nod, the little man closed the doors and set the rattling cage in motion.

When she stepped out of the elevator, she was surprised at how peaceful it was in the hallway. Of course, that was because Theo and the boys weren't around. Even though she missed their wisecracks, she could use the quiet to warm up in the alcove at the end of the corridor.

But as she neared Professor Schmieder's studio, she noticed the door wasn't all the way shut. That didn't make sense. Perhaps the policeman who had been here a few days ago had forgotten to lock up after himself. Or could the Towers' manager be showing the studio to a new tenant already, even though it had been the scene of the professor's passing just a week ago?

Aurora told herself she should keep on walking and stick with her original plan. But seeing the open door gave her the idea that she might be able to slip into the studio and exchange the professor's violin back with her own, with no one knowing that she had been the protector of the precious Gagliano for a few days. She tapped on the door to check if anyone was inside and didn't receive a response. After glancing up and down the hallway to make sure no one was watching, she stepped inside.

It took her a couple of seconds to find the light switch, but when she did Aurora was sorry she ever came in. The neat and tidy studio had been turned upside down. Sofa cushions were pulled from the frame, books toppled from the shelves, and music strewn across the piano and underneath.

What would the professor think? Strangers treating his belongings like so much rubbish to be tossed about. On instinct she walked across the room, placed the violin case on the closed piano lid, and started putting things in order.

As she stacked the pages of music she kept her eyes away from the window, even though the curtains were drawn back to reveal the gray January day. She moved on to the couch and fixed the cushions. There, that was better. Professor Schmieder would have been pleased.

With the housekeeping finished it was time to switch the violins, the reason she'd come into the studio in the first place. She retraced her steps from last Saturday morning: walking into the room, seeing the open window, setting down her violin near the door. But when she looked over, it wasn't there.

"That's strange," she said to herself, scanning the studio in case her violin had been moved. But she didn't see it anywhere. "What could have happened to it?"

Now she was in a quandary. She'd already given the studio a quick once-over while straightening. She didn't have time to search from top to bottom if she still wanted to get in a good warm-up.

"But the professor's violin is just sitting here," she said, walking back to the piano. "Maybe it wouldn't hurt if I played it just this once. Professor Schmieder might have even wanted me to." She touched the black case. "And then I'll run up here after the master class to look again for mine."

She opened the case and carefully lifted the professor's violin to her shoulder. She took out the bow and tightened the horsehair. She tested the A string for tuning, and the E string just to make sure. Even after only two notes, the beauty of the instrument's tone filled the room.

No wonder Professor Schmieder loved this violin so much, she thought.

After making a few adjustments to the chin rest, she faced the piano bench, where the professor used to sit during her lessons.

Closing her eyes, Aurora began vibrating the D string on the fingerboard with her left hand before gliding the bow into place with her right, ready to play the opening phrase of the "Romanze."

But the sound of the studio door shutting behind her abruptly interrupted the music. Could a draft have blown the door closed? She opened her eyes. No, the window wasn't open.

Maybe somebody out in the hall didn't want to hear her playing.

Then she heard the heavy breathing, inside the studio.

She whirled around with the bow still in midair. A figure was standing near the door with his back to her. He was wearing a too-large overcoat and a red wool cap pulled down over his ears.

"I'm sorry," said Aurora. "I didn't mean to bother anyone." She turned to lay the violin into the case. "I'll be out of here in a minute."

The lock in the door clicked.

Aurora flinched. Why was he locking the door if they were still inside?

"I'm playing in the master class downstairs." She hurried to put the bow away and latch the case. "You know, in Carnegie Hall."

She turned to face him.

"So I'll be going."

He was looking at her now, with an almost amused expression on his face.

He's the boy from the alley, she thought, the same one from the club where the professor used to play.

"You don't remember me, do ya?" he asked.

She shook her head, trying to play innocent.

"We met right here, just a week ago," he said. "After I saw you push the professor out the window."

He must not have noticed her at the Algonquin Hotel yesterday, during the debacle in the lobby with Theo and the boys.

"Who would have thought we'd meet here again?" He started to laugh.

"Since you mention it, I do remember you." She tried a little laugh of her own. "I just didn't recognize you right away."

"Now do you know me?" He pulled off his red cap.

With those ears, she could have picked him out anywhere.

"It's very nice seeing you again." Aurora made a move toward the door, bringing the violin with her. "But like I said, I need to get down to the concert hall."

"Not so fast, miss."

He planted himself squarely in her way.

"You've got something that belongs to me."

Aurora didn't dare take a peek at her watch, but she knew time was running short. Only she was worried about something more serious than playing in the master class. The young man's defiant stance was starting to scare her.

"I can't imagine what that would be," she said. "I mean, we hardly know each other. I don't even know your name."

"Sidney's my name." He took a step closer. "And that fiddle is mine." He pointed to the case she was carrying. "Where did you get it?"

"I don't know what you're talking about," she said. "My parents gave me this violin years ago."

"I don't think so," he said. "You know, you've caused me a heap of trouble."

Aurora took a deep breath.

"I should be going. They're waiting for me downstairs."

"Not so fast."

He reached for the light switch and flipped it off.

Aurora backed into the piano. From the shadows, she could see he was watching her like a cat watches a mouse. Waiting for the right moment to pounce.

"Why won't you let me leave?" she asked. "I haven't done anything to you."

"You took the old man's violin and left yours here," said Sidney.

"You mean the morning when Professor Schmieder ...?" She stopped short.

"That's right," said Sidney. "We thought the old man would be an easy mark, but he gave Miriam a real fight. She told me he hit his head on the piano and started bleeding all over the place."

Aurora cringed. The blood on the piano keys and the window sill.

"But somehow he got back up," said Sidney. "And then you know what happened to him next. You showed up after that."

Miriam was here when I came in? thought Aurora. *She must have been hiding in the back room.*

"Lucky you fainted and she was able to get out on the fire escape," said Sidney. "But you were right next to the fiddle, and she didn't have the nerve to grab it."

She probably stepped right over me, Aurora thought, shuddering.

"I had to come back in the afternoon after the police cleared out," said Sidney. "I took the violin I found in here, but how could I know it was the wrong one? When the boss saw that cheap imitation of yours, he was so mad he smashed it against the wall."

Aurora didn't have time to mourn her poor violin. Sidney was on a roll.

"Then we had another botched job this week," he said, "after we couldn't get out of the music guy's office with that other fancy violin."

Aurora held back a gasp. Her father had warned her about the violin thieves, and she and the boys had wondered why Miriam and Sidney would be friends with the professor. But if they knew him from the club, and how valuable his violin was …

The winter light from the window caught a glint from the blade of steel in Sidney's hand. This time Aurora's gasp was audible.

"Sit down over there," he said, using the knife to gesture toward the couch. "Leave the violin on the piano."

When Aurora didn't budge, he held up the knife and started toward her. She laid the case back down on the piano lid and crossed over to the other side of the room to sit on the sofa.

"Now that I've got the professor's violin back, that'll help me fix things with the boss." Sidney resumed his position at the door. "But I want the red glove, too. Where is it?"

Did he mean the red glove Miss Powell left in here last Saturday?

"This was the last place Miriam said she had both gloves with her," said Sidney. "But I couldn't find it when I came back for the fiddle, even though I tore up the room. I'm not leaving without it again."

Miriam had both gloves in the professor's studio, but Eddie only found one of them. The one with the money in it.

"Oh," said Aurora, and instantly regretted it.

"You do know what I'm talking about." The young's man rage spilled over. "Miriam came back with just one glove, the wrong one. She must have dropped the other one in here someplace, and I bet you know where it is."

Sidney started flipping the knife blade open and then closed. Aurora shivered with every snap.

"There was a hundred bucks in that glove. Miriam told me she put it in there."

Aurora wished she didn't know anything about the money, or the red gloves, or this whole awful business. How long was he going to keep her here? How could she convince him to let her go?

Very faintly she began to hear the sound of applause. Then she heard the opening measures of the Tchaikovsky concerto. The sound was coming up from Carnegie Hall through the heater vents.

The master class was starting. Mother, Father, and Grandmother would be staring at her vacant chair on the stage, wondering where she could be. Theo and the boys would be thinking the same thing. No one would guess she was all the way up on the fourth floor in Professor Schmieder's studio.

"My parents are going to be looking for me," said Aurora. "Why don't you let me leave and we'll forget about all this?"

"Not until you tell me where that money is." He stroked the knife blade along his pant leg.

She wanted to plug her ears so she couldn't hear the music from downstairs. But she was forced to listen as the violinist played on. Aurora closed her eyes and wished she could disappear.

Through the vents, she could hear another round of clapping and then a voice over the concert hall loudspeaker.

"Aurora Lewis. Aurora Lewis. Please come to the Carnegie Hall stage."

Suddenly cold metal pressed against her neck. Sidney was standing in front of her. One hand was pulling her head back by her hair, the other poised with the knife at her throat.

"I'm not standing around here all day."

Aurora fought the impulse to cry out. That would only make him angrier. But why wasn't somebody, anybody, looking for her?

"Come on." He wrapped her hair more tightly around his hand.

Aurora knew she had to come up with something. Time for that improvisation Professor Schmieder used to talk about.

"I'll tell you, but you have to move that knife away from me." She spoke as normally as she could. "Then I'll tell you everything."

He loosened his grip but barely drew back the knife.

"Where's the money?"

Aurora steeled herself.

"It's over there," she said.

"Where?"

He dropped his hold on her.

"In the violin case on the piano. I hid the money in there."

His eyes narrowed.

"You get it for me." He backed off a couple steps. "I don't want to get in any more trouble with the boss by messing with that fiddle."

"Aurora Lewis." Her name rang out over the ventilation system again. "Last call for Aurora Lewis. Please come to the stage."

Aurora rose from the sofa and walked over to the violin, stalling until she could figure out some way to escape.

"Hurry up," he said, with an anxious look.

She started rummaging around the pockets inside the case, but she couldn't keep him waiting forever. Somehow she'd have to distract him long enough to make a dash for the door.

"Are you gonna get that money for me or not?"

Then she saw the rosin. Professor Schmieder always kept a well-worn cake of the pressed powder in his case to rub on his violin bow.

"Here's the money," she said. "Right where I put it."

She opened the top of the rosin box.

Sidney couldn't contain his eagerness and stepped in close to her. Close enough for her to get a good aim at his eyes.

Chapter 30

AURORA DIDN'T WAIT TO see if the rosin hit its mark. The yelp of surprise followed by the shriek of pain was proof enough. As Sidney scrambled to get the sticky dust out of his eyes, his every motion created more burning. Aurora grabbed the violin case and rushed to the door.

With Sidney behind her yowling as loud as a wildcat, she fumbled with the lock. Then she heard pounding on other side of the door. Finally, someone was here to help her. Only she couldn't get to them.

"Aurora, are you in there?"

"Theo, is that you?" She started to sob. "Help me, please. He's got a knife."

"Aurora." Theo talked as if he was standing right beside her. "Stay calm and open the door."

Taking a deep breath, she turned the door handle one way and then the other. But just as she felt the lock release, she was grabbed from behind again, the blade pressing on her neck.

Theo rushed into the room when the door unlatched.

"Stay where you are." Sidney brandished the knife under Aurora's chin. "Or your girlfriend's gonna get sliced."

"Let her go." Theo spoke in his usual monotone. "You don't want to do anything you're going to regret."

"I'm long past that," said Sidney. "I just want to get out of here with my property, and she's gonna help."

Theo started toward them with measured steps.

"If you let her go," said Theo. "Nothing's going to happen to you. I'll make sure of it."

Aurora felt Sidney's body tense in anger, and his hold on her tighten.

"Don't come any closer."

"Just give me the knife," said Theo.

Aurora wanted to tell Theo to stop, but the look in his eye warned her against saying anything.

"Give me the knife," said Theo, stepping closer. "The police will be here any minute and this can all end quietly." He held out his hand. "With nobody getting hurt."

"You want it, do you?" Sidney suddenly loosened his grasp on Aurora, giving her a chance to twist away.

A bone-chilling roar erupted from Theo.

"Mother of …"

Sidney was standing over Theo's crumpled body, his knife already stained with blood, poised to strike again.

"Theo, you fool," she cried.

"What's going on in here?" Detective O'Shea was standing in the studio doorway, trying to catch his breath. Peering in from behind him, Aurora could see Bill and Eddie.

"Who turned off the lights?" asked the detective, flipping the switch.

Aurora turned to see Sidney opening the window behind the piano. He pulled himself up onto the sill, taking a good look outside. First to the right, then to the left, and then down.

"Wait for me, Miriam," he called out.

"Son, don't try it." Detective O'Shea bellowed. "Come off of there and we'll talk this over."

Sidney took a tentative step onto the ledge and then turned to them and sneered.

"You can all go to hell."

Sid's next step was a leap of faith. Too bad God wasn't watching.

Aurora didn't know what sounded worse. His scream of terror, or the dull thud of his body in the alleyway below.

Detective O'Shea took out a handkerchief and wiped his brow and then walked over to the window.

Aurora hurried to Theo, who was still hunched over near the piano.

"Did he really hurt you?" she asked, kneeling down beside him.

"It's not that bad," said Theo, holding his hand between his knees.

Aurora searched for something to stop the bleeding. Looking down, she saw the sash on her dress and pulled it off in two tugs.

"No, no," said Theo. "Don't ruin your dress."

"Theo, be quiet." Aurora got to work patching him up. Bill and Eddie were also there to help.

"I should have been here sooner," said Theo. "When I heard them call out your name at the master class, I knew you would never miss your chance to play. Then Maurice told me he brought you up here in the elevator."

"You were so brave," said Aurora. "You walked right up to him."

O'Shea stepped away from the window, talking to nobody in particular.

"He tried to get out by the fire escape and lost his footing on the ice. Fool of a kid."

He turned to Theo.

"Are you going to be okay?" he asked.

"He cut me pretty good," said Theo.

"Good thinking there, Miss Lewis, about wrapping his hand. But you'd better get to a doctor, young man. Just in case you need stitches."

Bill and Eddie helped Theo to his feet.

"How about you, Miss Lewis?" Detective O'Shea asked. "Did that fellow hurt you?"

Aurora shook her head. But without warning, tears began streaming down her face. She had been so worried about Theo, she'd forgotten how scared she was.

"He won't be bothering you again," said O'Shea.

Bill and Eddie headed to the window to see for themselves.

"Let's go over there, too," said Theo.

"Be careful." Aurora held on to him, keeping them both steady on their feet.

Looking down into the alley they saw Sidney sprawled onto the ground, lying face down. If Miriam had been waiting for him, she had since disappeared. Instead, a group of street boys was gathering around Sidney's body, poking at him with the tips of their boots. Then one of the ruffians pointed up at the Carnegie Towers and started shouting.

"There she is, she's the one that done it."

The rest of the boys turned to take a look.

"The girl with the red hair." The boy gestured in excitement. "In the window."

But this time Aurora Lewis didn't faint.

Chapter 31

"Thank goodness you're all right."

Aurora spun around to see Maud Powell standing just inside the studio. Her usually stylish hair was in a fluster, and her face was flushed.

"I left the auditorium as soon as the master class was over," said Miss Powell. "I had a feeling something had gone terribly wrong when you didn't show up. The elevator car was standing open, and the operator told me he'd brought you and then your friend up to the fourth floor." She looked closer at Theo's wrapped hand.

"Miss Lewis here is a fast thinker," said Detective O'Shea. "She kept this young man from bleeding to death."

"I'll be fine," said Theo. "Aurora stayed calm even when that guy grabbed ahold of her."

Maud Powell gave Aurora a curious look. "What guy?"

"Sidney," said Aurora.

"He fell out the window," added Eddie.

"Another one?" Miss Powell now looked really confused.

"Would you like to sit down?" Aurora gestured toward the couch. "Then we can tell you all about it, if it's okay with the detective."

O'Shea nodded. "All right, but just until my men get here. You'll have to clear out when they go over the place. And don't move anything."

Aurora and Maud Powell sat on the sofa while Theo took the chair next to them, still holding the makeshift wrap around his wounded hand. Detective O'Shea and the boys stepped in closer to hear about Aurora's chilling encounter with Sidney. From coming up to the fourth floor to practice and then finding the professor's studio unlocked, to Sidney trapping her inside and threatening her with the knife.

"He told me about how he and Miriam planned to steal the professor's violin," said Aurora.

"The elevator operator brought Miriam up here early last Saturday morning," said Theo. "Maybe she was going to get the violin while Sidney was waiting in the alley."

"They must have gotten mixed up in the thieving ring that's been going after musical instruments in the city," said Detective O'Shea.

"The same one that broke into my husband's office," said Miss Powell.

"Sidney said something about that, too," said Aurora.

"My guess is someone tipped him off about the worth of the professor's violin," said O'Shea. "Then he used Miriam to become friends with the old guy so she could get inside the studio."

"Only things didn't go as planned," said Aurora, trying not to imagine the scene of Miriam and the professor struggling by the window. "Miriam got away using the fire escape, but she left the professor's violin here. Sidney told me he had to come back on Saturday afternoon to get it."

"He's the one who must have ransacked the studio," said Theo. "Before the guys and I got here."

"But wait a minute," said Detective O'Shea. "If Sidney already had the professor's violin, why would he come back again today?"

"Because he took the wrong one," said Aurora.

All eyes turned to her.

"Miss Lewis, would you care to explain?" asked O'Shea.

Without a word, Aurora stood up from the sofa and walked over to where she had laid the violin case back down on the closed piano lid. She opened it and gently took out the instrument.

Miss Powell rose to join her. "The Gagliano," she said quietly.

Aurora turned to Detective O'Shea.

"I must have picked up the professor's violin by accident last Saturday," she said. "I didn't even know I had it until a couple days ago. I was hoping I'd be able to switch it back with mine without anyone knowing." She sneaked a glance at Theo. "I didn't want anyone to think I'd taken the professor's violin on purpose, and that I might have had a reason to harm him."

"It's not Aurora's fault, Detective." Bill spoke up. "I handed her that violin. I found it right next to where she fainted by the piano. I just assumed it was hers. If there's anyone to blame, it should be me."

Aurora admired Bill for standing up for her, but she knew she should have told someone once she had discovered the mistake.

"Well, you both probably saved that violin," said Detective O'Shea. "Although Miss Lewis, you put yourself in a dangerous position by not telling anyone about it."

"I can see that now," said Aurora. "I don't know what would have happened if Theo didn't show up."

Bill gave Theo a pat on the back. "And we were right behind you, old man."

"Yeah, right," said Theo. "Why did you come up to the fourth floor anyway? I just said I was going to check on Aurora."

"When you didn't come back and Aurora never showed on stage, we knew something was happening," said Bill. "We left the auditorium to find you and saw Detective O'Shea heading up the stairs to the Towers."

"I thought there might be some trouble at the class because of the goings-on with Professor Schmieder." O'Shea patted his right hip, revealing the outline of a gun holster. "But when I saw that Aurora was missing, I realized I should have kept an eye on the professor's studio, too. Only the elevator was taking too long to get back to the lobby." His hand rose to his chest. "Hoofing it up those stairs just about did me in."

He stepped toward the window and gazed down into the alley. "Looks like Daley just got here." He whistled to get officer's attention. "Sergeant, come up to the fourth floor when you're done down there."

"Why did you come here last Saturday morning, Miss Powell?" asked Theo.

Maud took a deep breath.

"I was having second thoughts about how things had ended between Anton and me the evening before," she said. "Since I'd been a student of his in Heidelberg, he came by the hall asking me for money. But I stopped studying with him all those years ago because he wouldn't take me seriously as a musician, because I'm a woman."

"Is that why the Paganini 'Romanze' has sad memories for you?" asked Aurora. "Because of its association with Professor Schmieder?"

Miss Powell nodded. "I was playing his arrangement of the 'Romanze' before we had our big argument. I stormed out of his studio and Anton swore after me that I'd never amount to anything more than a parlor violinist. Then after I got back to the United States, it almost seemed like he'd put a curse on me. I couldn't get anyone to listen to me play until I finally walked into the New York Philharmonic and insisted the conductor give me a chance."

"That conductor was Theodore Thomas," said Aurora, remembering Miss Powell's biography in the concert program.

"Maestro Thomas was a wonderful gentleman," said Miss Powell. "He asked me to perform the Bruch concerto at the very next orchestra concert, and I've had a successful career ever since." She paused. "That's why, after I had a chance to calm down about seeing Anton again, I wanted to make amends. After all, he'd been a good teacher, even though he was outdated in his thinking."

"Professor Schmieder was old-fashioned in a lot of ways," said Aurora. "But he was always encouraging to me about becoming a professional musician."

"Then maybe you'll be the one to turn the Paganini curse into a charm," said Maud.

Aurora smiled. She'd like to think something good might come out of this week of misfortune.

"What happened when you saw the professor, Miss Powell?" asked Theo, bringing her back to her narrative.

"Oh, I was only here for a few minutes." She looked around the room. "We talked about the old days, and then I offered him the money. But he didn't take it."

"He didn't?" asked Theo. "After all that?"

"Not at first. In fact, he wanted to sell me his violin. But of course I couldn't take his livelihood away from him, so he finally accepted the money. He was terribly grateful, and, I think, embarrassed. I left quickly after that, because it was so awkward."

"Was there anyone else in here while you were talking to Professor Schmieder?" asked O'Shea.

"No, just the two of us." She paused. "Except I did hear a rustling sound coming from back there." She pointed toward the curtained-off alcove. "I said something about it, but Anton told me the window was broken and it was just the wind."

"Miriam must have been in the back room while you and Professor Schmieder were talking," said Aurora. "She was here to take the violin, but then she saw you give him the money. She got it away from him somehow and tucked the bills into one of your gloves."

"I guess I was in quite a state when I left," said Miss Powell. "I didn't notice my gloves were missing until later, and I didn't know where I'd left them."

"Sidney told me he was plenty angry at Miriam when she showed up with the wrong glove," said Aurora. "He figured she must have left the other one in here. The one Eddie found with the money in it."

"Where's the money now?" asked O'Shea.

"We kept it nice and safe," said Eddie with a grimace. "Theo made sure of that."

"Then this must be the second glove to the pair," said Detective O'Shea, taking it from his pocket. "Miriam dropped it on the sidewalk outside Finkelstein's."

"Does it a have a *T* monogrammed on the cuff?" asked Aurora, with a smile toward Theo.

"Now that you mention it." The detective took a look. "It does. I guess I never noticed that before."

"*T* for Turner," said Maud.

"I'd like to keep this for a while longer, Mrs. Turner, if you don't mind," said O'Shea. "I was going to ask Miriam about it if I saw her again. Only now we'll have a lot more to discuss once we have her in custody."

No one talked for a few moments until Eddie spoke up.

"But there's something I still don't understand," he said. "If Aurora had the professor's fiddle all this time, where's hers?"

Until now, she had forgotten about the tragic fate of her own violin.

"If what Sidney said is true, it ended up somewhere broken into little pieces," said Aurora.

"Oh, I'm so sorry," said Miss Powell. "But I'm sure we can find you another one."

"Maybe the detective will let you keep on borrowing the professor's," said Eddie.

"I would, but it's not up to me," said O'Shea. "If Schmieder didn't have any heirs, everything will go to auction to pay off his bills. His fiddle might end up in a museum somewhere."

"That would be a terrible shame," said Aurora, admiring the instrument. "A fine violin needs to be played, not just looked at."

The room fell quiet again, until an earsplitting summons shattered the silence.

"Aurora Elizabeth Lewis."

That voice could only belong to one person.

Aurora looked toward the studio door. Mother stood there with Father, Grandmother, and Maurice, the elevator operator, behind her.

"Ma'am, I need to get back to work now," said Maurice, although he didn't dare budge until Mother gave him permission.

"All right." She waved him away. "We don't need you anymore."

Maurice was gone in a flash.

"Aurora, you'd better have a good reason why you weren't on that stage today," said Mother. "I see that even Miss Powell had to come looking for you. And what is that policeman doing here?" Then her eyes scanned over to Bill and Eddie, finally resting on Theo and the blood-soaked green sash wrapped around his hand.

Aurora groaned inside. She had even more explaining to do now.

But she didn't have to deal with Mother on her own this time. Detective O'Shea stepped forward to shake her father's hand. He nodded toward Grandmother and then turned to Mother.

"Mrs. Lewis, your daughter was a very brave girl today." He gently guided her away from the studio, with Father and Grandmother following. "You should be very proud of her." The detective's voice grew fainter as they headed down the hallway.

Aurora sighed with relief. She would have never expected to think this way about him, but she was thankful for Detective O'Shea.

"We should go, too," said Eddie. "They're going to be in here soon to investigate." He glanced at the open window. "Besides, this place gives me the creeps."

"Me too," said Bill.

"Aurora," said Miss Powell, once they were in the hallway. "I want you to have a chance to make up for missing the master class today. You can come to my house in Great Neck for a private lesson. Just you and me. And I'll get working on finding you another violin."

"Really?" asked Aurora, hardly able to speak. "That ... that would be great."

"So it's settled. I'll be in touch," said Maud. Then she turned to Theo before leaving. "You need to get that hand looked at right away, young man."

"Don't worry, Miss Powell," said Bill. "We'll get him to the doctor."

"I just want to make sure Aurora's all right before we go," said Theo. "I'll meet you guys by the elevator."

At first Bill and Eddie didn't get the hint.

"I'll be over there in a minute," said Theo, in a stronger voice.

Then they got the message and started walking away.

"What's the matter?" asked Aurora, once the others were out of earshot. "Of course I'm okay, you're the one who's hurt."

Theo took a long look at her. "I need to talk to you about something."

She was struck by the seriousness in his voice.

"If it's about my violin, I'm sure I'll get another one," she said. "Maybe even a better one with Miss Powell's help."

"It's not about your violin, although I'm glad you're not too upset," said Theo. "I need to tell you something." He stopped.

"What is it, Theo?" she asked.

"I need to tell you that I'm moving out to California in a few weeks." He rushed through the words. "Once I turn eighteen."

Aurora thought she hadn't heard him correctly.

"California?"

"I've been planning this for months," he said.

"But what's out there?" She silently hoped he wouldn't answer that there was another girl.

"The movie industry is going to be big in California, and I want to get in on the start of it," said Theo, his face filled with excitement. "There's sunshine all year round for filming, and companies from New York are already talking about building movie studios as big as whole city blocks."

Aurora still wasn't getting what he was saying.

"But what about—"

"You and me?" Theo finished her sentence. "A week ago, I was too scared even to talk to you. Today you're the only reason I would stay."

Then why don't you? she wanted to ask.

"You deserve the best, Aurora," said Theo. "I'm going to give it to you someday. That's why I have to leave. Hollywood is the future for me."

He leaned over to whisper in her ear.

"For both of us."

Chapter 32

AURORA SETTLED INTO HER favorite reading nook hidden away from the Osborne's front lobby. Usually on a warm spring day she would have taken her time walking home from school, talking with her friends about their plans for summer vacation or the latest dresses they had seen in the fashion magazines.

But this afternoon she hurried to pack up her books as soon as the school bell rang and then practically ran down Fifty-Seventh Street to reach her building. Only she didn't go upstairs, not just yet.

She carefully took out the long white envelope she'd kept safe all day in her book bag. Grandmother had put the letter on her bed after supper last night and Aurora slept with it under her pillow, unopened. To dream a little longer of what might be inside.

This was the first letter she had received from Theo since their parting nearly four months earlier. She'd seen the other two boys at the Carnegie Towers a few times since then. Naturally Bill bragged about how he would use his experience tangling with the violin thief when the right acting part came along, while Eddie eagerly told her he would be joining Theo in California after the school term ended, to make movies and soak up the sun.

After holding the letter for a few more minutes, she was finally ready to read it. Gently unfolding the single sheet of paper, she thought of how Theo must have taken the time to crease it just right. The careful printing on the envelope was repeated inside, striking for its precision and brevity. For once she wished Theo could have been more like Eddie and Bill, with more to say rather than less.

Theo started the letter by telling her he'd been hired on as a production assistant at the fledgling Nestor Studios. He was working on one-reel westerns now but was hoping to get assigned to the drama films department soon. Then he asked how her violin studies were going, and if she had been to any Philharmonic concerts lately. Only in his last few sentences did he mention what Aurora had been waiting to hear. Being Theo, he wrote it in his matter-of-fact way.

"I know your school semester ends later this month and you are looking forward to what lies ahead. I wish I could ask you to come to California, but that wouldn't be fair. I'm not ready to support you, and you have so much more to learn about your own life. You are a very talented violinist, and more important, a very fine girl. I wish you the best in whatever you decide to do. I remain most faithfully yours, Theo."

If Aurora was prone to tears, now would be the time. Instead, she carefully folded the letter and put it back in the envelope. Gathering up her belongings, she followed the winding passageway to the lobby. She would cry herself to sleep tonight. Right now, she had a violin lesson to get ready for.

Once a month Aurora took the train, by herself, from the city to Miss Powell's home on Long Island. Playing the lovely violin Miss Powell helped find for her, Aurora spent the afternoon going through the masterworks of Mozart and Beethoven, along with new pieces by American composers, including women composers like Amy Beach.

During her lesson last month, Miss Powell had asked Aurora about her plans to continue her training after she graduated from high school. She'd even suggested that Aurora move to Paris, which was becoming the center of all things artistic and a magnet for young American musicians, writers, and painters.

At the time Aurora dismissed the idea, it seemed so impossible. But now she wasn't as sure.

She started climbing the staircase that led up to her family's apartment.

Things were better at home. Mother and Father had settled into a comfortable truce. No more ultimatums or threats to leave. It was almost as if they were getting to know each other again.

Grandmother was moving a little slower but was as mischievous as always. She would miss Aurora if she went away to study, but would never consider holding her granddaughter back from what would truly make her happy.

Aurora paused when she reached the top of the stairs.

Maybe it was time to make the next decision about her own life.

She smiled to herself.

But she would think about that another day.

—THE END—

CPSIA information can be obtained at www.ICGtesting.com
Printed in the USA
LVOW12s1740040913

350979LV00006B/1221/P